We Trade Our Night for Someone Else's Day

We Trade Our Night for Someone Else's Day

IVANA BODROŽIĆ

translated by Ellen Elias-Bursać

Seven Stories Press
New York • Oakland

Seven Stories Press
140 Watts Street
New York, NY 10013
sevenstories.com

College professors and high school and middle school teachers may order free examination copies of Seven Stories Press books. To order, visit www.sevenstories.com, or fax request on school letterhead to (212) 226-1411.

Library of Congress Cataloging-in-Publication Data

Names: Simić Bodrožić, Ivana, 1982- author. | Elias-Bursać, Ellen, translator.
Title: We trade our night for someone else's day / Ivana Bodrožić ; [translated by Ellen Elias-Bursać].
Other titles: Rupa. English
Description: New York, NY : Seven Stories Press, [2021]
Identifiers: LCCN 2020044885 (print) | LCCN 2020044886 (ebook) | ISBN 9781644210482 (trade paperback) | ISBN 9781644210499 (ebook)
Subjects: LCSH: Vukovar (Croatia)--Fiction. | GSAFD: Suspense fiction.
Classification: LCC PG1620.29.I44 R8713 2021 (print) | LCC PG1620.29.I44 (ebook) | DDC 891.8/336--dc23
LC record available at https://lccn.loc.gov/2020044885
LC ebook record available at https://lccn.loc.gov/2020044886

Printed in the United States of America

9 8 7 6 5 4 3 2 1

Contents

Part One

HOLE

I.

Hands

finger a fold on the silken skirt
let the fingernail rip to pain

now (fall 2010)

"The worst part is realizing you can't open the door from the inside," was the first thing she said. Then she fixed her gaze on the gray linoleum floor and spent a long time picking at the cuticle around her fingernail, her skinned elbows propped on the school desk. On her left pinkie and ring finger she was still wearing fake nails, so she hadn't been there long. There were moments when the look on her face was bemused, as if she'd surfaced, mystified, from another time, but this quickly faded to stiffness and a dull gaze. Nora had no idea how to kickstart the conversation, and even less how to get close to her after all the salacious, tragic, twisted stories of pedophilia the papers had been printing about her for weeks. She hadn't expected her to look like this—a shapely blonde with light eyes in the Požega prison visitors' lounge. Nora would have trusted this woman to

9

look after her child—if she'd had a child—without a second thought while she ran an errand. She'd spent hours poring over the photos peddled to the tabloids by shocked relatives and people who until recently had been this woman's friends: a snapshot of her wrapped in a sarong, out with her husband at the river island beach, squinting into the sun and grinning at the person behind the camera; then another shot of her, head bowed, wearing a jacket with sleeves reaching down below her wrists, being escorted out of the building while the old ladies peered out of their windows, their elbows planted on brightly colored cushions; and, finally, a third one of her standing, contrite, in the modest courtroom of the county court. In this last picture, published on the front page the previous week, Nora thought she saw (had she merely imagined this?) a jeer playing around the woman's tightly pressed lips. "This dragon-lady story is the sort of plum you don't get every day," said the editor of the paper as he urged her to take on the job, but somewhere beneath his coercive, wheedling veneer she sniffed the sleaze of the system in which she lived and worked. The editor supported her male colleagues without a blink, and he spoke to them, even when they were junior to her, with courtesy and respect, while whenever anybody dropped by the office he dispatched Nora to fetch the coffees, even though she was better educated and more competent than the men. He occasionally spoke with admiration for the slick criminals in politics and others who boasted of their reputations as war criminals while they strutted around, flashing their folksy charm. He thought they were badass, even if he didn't share their politics. This made Nora sick. She'd rather be writing about other things; she ached to have a go at the people at the top, to expose the system, which stank like a fish from the head. She would have preferred to keep away from this desperate-housewives woman who'd snapped and murdered her husband. Nora was vying with a colleague to dig up dirt on the mayor of the city, who had offered to bribe a city councillor from the opposition party; the councillor had recorded their conversation and made the recording public. But instead, Nora was assigned the desperate housewife. Everybody already knew the facts—they'd been chewed over in several dailies. K. G.—a teacher at the city's general and vocational high school—had hooked up with, or possibly seduced, D. V., a seventeen-year-old student. After they'd been together a few months, the teacher talked the boy into killing her husband. Three shots to the chest and head, pools of blood; the neighbors heard the screams. True love is so poignant. At first the alibi was a break-in, then self-defense, but soon the lovers confessed. There was no conclusive proof that he'd pulled the trigger, so the boy was released from jail on the condition that he be committed to a mental health institution for many years. K. G. made no comment—and now she couldn't open the door from the inside. It appeared to be the logical outcome.

"I'm not recording this; I've come to see you, and, as you probably know, I'm a reporter; I'd like to hear your side of the story, that's all," Nora blurted out.

"Are you married?" Kristina asked, her voice tired, never looking up from her nails.

Nora paused, weighing whether to marry herself off on the spot to keep the conversation going, but instead she opted for sincerity. "No, I'm not. I was with someone, but"—then she broke off, midsentence, wondering what it was about this woman that she'd nearly begun to confide in her about her own life.

"What point is there, then, in telling you?"

"Well, I don't know. How did it all begin?" She pushed on, knowing this was her only chance.

"How did what begin?" Kristina laughed and shook her head. Nora could see that once something like this has happened, the person to whom it happened no longer speaks the same language other people speak. One of the two women talking in the lounge was behind bars, while the other was free and independent. But Kristina had nothing left to lose, so she could allow herself everything, while Nora still had everything to lose: the interview, her freedom, her job, her resilience, her solitude. Kristina laughed, while Nora kept her mouth shut— and weighed every word spoken to Krstina and everybody else. Somewhere, beneath the surface, this ordinary, banal, and tawdry prison could actually free you. The pressure that rose from Nora's chest to her throat every evening was released, strangely, by Kristina's harsh barks of laughter; yes, freed.

"I wanted Ante dead, I did, I did. Really . . . Ever since we moved back to the city. I had the whole thing down to a science, every evening when he came home and I heard the key in the lock. Whether he was drunk or not—I could tell by how he turned the key. And once it turned, hop to it, girl, God help us. Out of bed with you. It was even worse if I pretended to be sleeping. I jumped as high as the roof without him so much as lifting a finger. Never once in all our fifteen years did he hit me; ha! But it was: dance me a jig! Sing me the anthem; swear,

swear to me up and down that you've no clue where your father is. Till he dropped off to sleep in my lap before dawn, slobbering, drenched in sweat, a wreck. 'You're all I have,' he'd sob. The motherfucker." Here Kristina stopped. Here, where she'd only just begun—but the images shimmied before Nora's eyes, and she couldn't work out how to keep moving forward with any sort of reasonable question. She didn't dare take up paper and pencil; all of this had to be committed to memory.

"So, he abused you?" and after she'd uttered the words she knew this was a mistake; her question was all wrong, way off base and so insulting, even to a woman who'd just been convicted of murder. But she didn't want to approach the story the same way the right-wing tabloids and Serbian papers had been doing, the way most of the local papers except the official press had done. Their fangs were bared, the blood dribbling down their chins, especially at the news that Kristina was a Croatian-language teacher for students who were ethnic Serbs. She was Croatian, married to a Croat; her husband, Ante, was a war veteran—a war invalid, a former prison-camp internee. Meanwhile, Dejan, her teenage lover, was from a Serbian family, born in the city in 1993, while it was still under Serbian occupation. Dejan's grandfather was one of the leaders of the Serbian territorial defense, the Chetniks, who scuttled off like cockroaches after Eastern Slavonia—the region they'd occupied by force—was reintegrated peacefully into Croatia three years after the war. When Kristina spoke of her return with Ante to the city after reintegration, she was referring to a time when Dejan was still only six or seven. So what did Ante making her dance a jig and Kristina's lost father have to do with any of this? In response to her question about abuse, Kristina shot Nora a sharp glance that could easily be read as: *Stupid woman, so what if I have all the time in the world? Don't waste it.*

They stopped speaking. Nora broke out in a cold sweat; she could tell her forehead shone and felt the hairs gluing themselves to her neck. As so many times before, she knew she didn't have what it took, so she shut her eyes, wondering how much longer things could go on like this. She longed to do right by the story; she couldn't bear to be one more in the parade of reporters smearing this woman, penning an article and going on with their lives. She often felt that way, to be honest, when faced with almost any story involving people. She didn't have the stomach to hold her nose and poke at the half-putrid flesh. She had no backbone; she'd pull back just when she should be getting the story. When she reached the point where ideas took precedence over people—the essence of sensationalism—she shut her eyes and took herself off to the Drava riverbanks of her girlhood. Her, her father, her mother. The smell of their gray terrier's wet fur and the roasting corn, all the river's shades of August green. Arching over the river, the bridge spanning the two banks, the place where everything stopped. *Cut.*

Kristina, her gnawed hangnails caked in blood. Their time was up, and soon Nora would have to stand up and walk out of the Požega women's correctional facility. The policewoman had already risen from her chair and was pacing nervously back and forth around the room, glancing pointedly at her watch. Nora realized that Kristina wouldn't be saying much more, that she'd lost all desire to rehash the story.

"Fine, thanks for your time," Nora managed to say. "Take care," she added.

Kristina looked over at her and then went back, absently, to her nails. She was trying to reattach one of the ones that had come loose, licking it and pressing down hard. This was the last image Nora took away with her. She hoped against hope that this one visit would suffice, that she'd extract a few sturdy, logically grounded facts that would then allow her to get something down on paper and polish the story for style. She hoped she wouldn't have to venture into the city or, if she did, that she wouldn't have to linger long, interviewing witnesses. They'd already said everything, anyway; they'd been waiting in line during the investigation to have their say. People like that always knew everything. Of course, from what she'd gleaned in the two hours spent over the torn fingernails, there was a story here, a story about silence and anguish, but this story was of interest to no one else but her, and least of all her editor. Something here was pulling Nora in, however, even more than she'd expected. She jotted down incoherent sentences in her notebook as soon as she left, shut her eyes tight, shook her head, and decided to see when there was a bus leaving Požega for the city that afternoon.

       ℘   ℘   ℘

Forget this city

and forget this city
forget this city
forget this city

Many years ago, she'd had a friend in the city. They met poolside, during the summer when they both turned eleven. She remembered how one evening, after a whole day spent together, their shoulders sunburned and eyes red from the chlorine, they'd traded addresses, hugged for a long time in their wet swimsuits, and then, for a few months, they'd written each other regularly. That same last day, a boy had gone missing from the city pool, and this was part of what had kept them close. They remembered him, too, or at least talked each other into believing he'd been swimming with friends right near them. When the pool began to empty out as kids left to go home, Dražen was nowhere to be found. His towel, wristwatch, and gnawed peach pits were still there by the railing. The lifeguards quickly drained the Olympic-size pool, thinking he'd drowned, but no body was found. It was only weeks later, entirely by chance, when the Danube swelled with autumn rains, that a rock slid out from the noose someone had tied around the child's neck, and the bloated corpse rose to the surface.

Children began disappearing from the city that summer as never before. Rumors made the rounds about a white van parked out in front of the school and a beautiful woman who sneaked out from the van to entice kids with candy; about people roaming the streets at night dressed in black, seeking children; about the hearts and kidneys they cut from them. The two girls wrote to each other about all these things, crafted their own detective story and believed they were the only ones who could solve the mystery. The last letter Nora wrote her friend was when the war had already begun—about ankle boot–style shoes with inch-high heels she'd bought at the Novska open-air market for five hundred Croatian dinars—but her letter was returned to her, undeliverable. Never again did she hear from her summertime friend, or from the many others she'd known back then, some of them really close friends. As the bus pulled into the station she remembered that her friend's father had worked at Hotel Danube, the only hotel in town when she was a child. She hoped it was still standing. She knew she wouldn't be able to find anyone to interview at eight o'clock at night except random passersby, if there was anyone passing by at random. What she needed was a little peace of mind and quiet so she could cobble together a plan for the next day and, if nothing else, identify the relatives and acquaintances who still had doubts from a list she'd been given by colleagues from the other newspapers.

There was almost nobody at the station; hers was probably the last bus to pull in for the night, bringing Nora and three other passengers. None of them were met. She looked over at the two peeling station benches. A drunk was nodding off on one, cracking open an eye every so often. By Platform One a man suddenly hopped to his feet from the other bench and started walking toward her. He seemed ordinary enough, in jeans and a leather jacket, frowning, maybe in his early forties. He had no obvious reason for approaching her. When he was only two steps away she veered to step around him, with her small suitcase in one hand and a backpack on her back, but he stood in front of her and gave no ground, determined to get her attention. Their eyes met for a second. He was tall and heavyset, his hands in his pockets, blocking her view of the city, which she was comparing mentally with her childhood memories.

"Taxi," was all he said, his voice clean and dark.

"Ah," sighed Nora, shaking her head, "I'm not going far; thanks."

He merely nodded and went on to his car; he'd probably been waiting for the last passengers to disembark. Nora watched him unlock an old white Opel Corsa that had no taxi sign on the roof but, despite rust spots here and there, seemed well enough maintained. He stubbed out his cigarette as he got in, slid the key into the ignition, and shifted into reverse. Only then did it occur to Nora that she could have asked him a few questions.

Hotel Danube was no longer the only hotel in town, but it was the only one where she knew she'd find a room her editor would pay for. The newer Hotel Lav, just a few hundred feet off, boasted four stars and was on the brink of bankruptcy, much like the rest of Croatia. Government ministers came here for anniversaries, the occasional businessmen showed up, and potential investors dragged themselves all the way to this city at the easternmost edge of the country. The place was a hard sell. Why trek to this inland city on the Danube when they could go to charming Istria, by the sea? Everything here had sunk into a black hole: money, people, hotels, children, initiatives, projects.

For months there'd been predictions swirling of a rosy future, and rumors of billions scheduled to materialize at any minute from a mysterious Chinese investor for a project known as The Port, the construction of a new canal between the Danube and the Sava riverways. Tales were spun about a tariff-free zone. For several decades now in the port zone—serving both Croatia and Serbia, the two countries the city belonged to—mournful, rusty tugboats had been moored next to towering cranes, which mostly went unused, although the port was one of the few local businesses that was not losing money. Every twenty to thirty years, a bona fide head of state would show up and wave from the deck of the good ship *Golubica*, deliver the baton for a nationwide annual relay race, declare an end to the war, or offer a formal apology for the latest bloody spree in this oh-so-peaceful place.

Hotel Danube might have looked shabby that autumn evening, but the price was right. Nora preferred to avoid dwelling on its past, the goings-on during the war, the people who'd stayed there. All she cared about was having a place to sleep so that the next day, as early as possible, she could do her interviews, setting aside all that really interested her to focus on the love story with its tragic denouement.

2.

Someone's watching us

everything's not lost
there's something I have gained

before (spring 2010)

"Tell me, Brigita, what's worrying you? I am no goldfish granting magic wishes, but there's plenty I can do."

"What can you do? I mean, specifics."

"When are you up for reelection?"

"I am all set for the next three years, as far as that goes. What I want to know is what I'll get if I endorse you. What you get is obvious enough: four more years, the port . . . But what about me? What about my family friends? I mean, my posse, if I cross the aisle to support you . . . And not just that; you know how they see things."

"Fine, Brigita, look: I've moved Ante now; he runs that association and has a vote. He won't cause any more trouble, and when he raises his hand in support, everyone else will follow suit, like dogs peeing in a row. You're fighting for the city, everyone can see that, and you're fighting by supporting me, even though I'm across the aisle. Nobody has the right to call you to account—"

"Sure, sure, we're all fighting for the same things, but what do I get except a kick in the teeth for colluding with the enemy?"

"Look, bringing you onto the supervisory board will be a breeze. I'm a member of the port board now, and I'm not compensated. But as soon as I have the election in hand, I'll withdraw and pass the chair on to you, Brigita. There's an easy two-thousand-kuna honorarium there. And other tasty opportunities will come your way! When we get to nominations, you'll move ahead—a seat on the Commission for European Integration; you'll fly two, three times a month to Brussels. There'll be other opportunities. Per diems. All the rest. And I should tell you . . ."

"Yes?"

"Our mutual benefit aside, you're perfect for it."

"Listen, I'm embarrassed to raise this, but I've heard people all over town are saying my appointment is a done deal. I find this a little . . . you know . . . It makes me look bad. I thought our arrangements were private."

"Brigita, I'll say this just once. They're shooting in the dark, wild guesses. You're a smart cookie. And I, as mayor, say that because unlike other men who may see work with women differently, I adore women, and that's my problem. . . . I believe friendship functions far better between women and men."

"No such thing."

"Friends? A man and a woman?"

"No such thing."

"Okay, well, I disagree with you there, but you're young yet; you'll figure this out for yourself."

"I'll sleep on your offer and be in touch."

"Of course. I look forward to hearing from you."

Brigita hung up and switched off her recorder. She got up from the leather desk chair in her high school principal's office and stood by the window, half-hidden behind the thick, dark-red curtain. There were teenagers in the schoolyard, standing in groups and smoking. They weren't socializing across the chain-link fence that split the playground in two, and only now and then, when cigarettes passed through the links, did their generational solidarity override the divide. A mere fifteen miles away, neighboring Osijek had none of these problems, but nobody in the city gave a thought anymore to how ridiculous the divisions were. Irritating nonprofit organizations came to visit from time to time, trekking through the elementary and secondary schools; there were associations founded by Scandinavians to promote reconciliation, innovative educational models, studies done of the region, shared classrooms. From the nonprofits Brigita heard sob stories like one about two little boys named David who'd grown up in the same apartment building and loved playing together until they started going to day care, where the playground was split down the middle by a fence into the Serbian and Croatian play areas, so they sat on either side of it for days, playing through the links. She was barely able to push the do-gooders out of her office. The civil associations were oh-so-sensitive, she thought while listening to their whiny presentations about the rights of children and transgenerational trauma. She had not, herself, been keen on the chain-link-fence approach, but if there was no other way, order and discipline had to be maintained.

Brigita Arsovska had moved to the city from Zagreb not long after the peaceful reintegration, when an opportunity for a position came up in an at-risk school, with all the associated privileges. But even with the benefits package to sweeten the deal, a person had to have a strong stomach for work in the city. It had taken twenty-seven excavators trundling through the streets to clear away the rubble from the ruins of buildings, sometimes mixed with human bones. Her father, a retired officer of the Yugoslav People's Army, had moved the family to Zagreb from Macedonia. She and her mother and father lived in an apartment in New Zagreb, and their day began early, at 5:00 a.m., with Pavle Arsovski's hacking coughs. While her mother polished his boots, Brigita served her father breakfast in the early-morning gloom, as she'd done as far back as she could remember. He was always silent, sometimes more aggressive, sometimes less. He demanded submission, discipline, and quiet. And his only daughter often failed to meet these three demands. Her mother noticed very early on that Brigita was wont to steal away and lacked respect for authority, so at least for that she appreciated Pavle's fierce parenting. When Brigita was in the eighth grade, she'd load her pockets up with eye shadow and eyeliner she'd shoplifted and go out for a walk through the Travno neighborhood. Under her woolen sweater she'd wear a close-fitting T-shirt she'd borrowed from a classmate. Once, her father saw her sitting on a park bench with a group of kids who were guzzling Badel cognac. He said nothing, but she jumped up and walked three steps behind him to their apartment. By the time she reached the elevator she'd already wet herself, and she didn't go to school for the next five days.

A few years later, Pavle began coughing harder, louder, more often, until tiny red droplets became an everyday sight on the white bathroom tiles. The cancer advanced quickly; Brigita slept in until 9:00 a.m. the morning after the funeral, waking up more rested than she'd ever felt. The day was sunny. When she came into the little dining room where her mother served breakfast, she met her mother's lost gaze.

Brigita wanted everything, but more than anything she wanted money. Good hard cash, full of promise, money that could grant her wishes, money that didn't discriminate, that forced people's true nature out in the open; from the bottom of her heart she wanted money. And with it, she wanted fun.

In 1991, just as the war was breaking out, she enrolled at the Zagreb Teacher Education Academy; she knew she'd need some sort of higher education if she was to live up to her ambitions. That very evening she went right across the street from the academy to the swanky InterContinental hotel. This was one of the many casinos in the capital city with an elite clientele and the requisite massage parlors. Brigita's plan was to study by day and work as a croupier by night. She landed the job there and then. She was nineteen and a striking beauty with slightly exotic, Grecian features, long black hair, a slender face, and dark, almond-shaped eyes. Her petite, hooked nose only enhanced her charm, and she was quickly put in charge of the tables with the high rollers. She was eloquent, even seductive, and though she didn't sleep at night and slept only two to three hours during the day, she had the kind of bounce that always gave her an arresting appeal.

It was only a matter of time before she found herself a boyfriend with a pistol tucked in his belt. Schweppes showed up in her life in 1992. He was the Boss's sidekick, and five years later, during the flurry of revenge killings among the kingpins of the underworld, Schweppes, who'd surfaced here and there in the war zones, vanished altogether.

The existence of the criminal network was never proved, and the rest of the gangsters cleaned up their act and forged a legal footing for their businesses. In the corner of the casino with the best view of the tables sat the Boss, whose favorite pastime was smacking croupiers with a baseball bat whenever one of them began to lose. He kept it by the table leg in a gilded umbrella stand. Those first war years were the most exhilarating. Organized crime flourished, hand in hand with the emerging state. The criminal underworld, with the casino as its outlet, rose to the surface with the blessings of the highest echelons of government. The relationship was reciprocal. While the gangsters dressed up as army generals by day, plundered diamonds that had been locked away in safes, and dabbled in matters of state over coffee, the army generals unclasped their medals by night, pulled on their balaclavas, and went underground. Not long after the new powermongers consolidated their positions, bloody clashes erupted, and there was a savage reckoning—for humiliations never forgotten, the festering insult. Blood was the color of the 1990s. What with all the decomposed bodies, holes in heads, sundered limbs—there was nowhere to go. Killing was the only option left.

$$\text{\small ❦ \quad ❦ \quad ❦}$$

The real world around me
I reach out
I touch things

A soft knock came through the thick office door padded in quilted leather. Brigita quickly slipped the tape recorder into a drawer and sat down at her desk. Professor Kristina Gelo scanned the room to see if the principal was alone.

"May I?" she asked from the doorway.

"Come right in. Sit down, please. Is class out?"

"Yes." Kristina smiled and dropped her hands with their carefully manicured nails into her lap. "But this high-pressure weather system is more than I can handle. My head's throbbing; there are no seasons anymore."

"You're so right about that; I never know what to wear," agreed Brigita, and then she coughed and went on, a little softer but enunciating clearly, "Do you know why I called you in?"

"I think so." Kristina rolled her eyes. "I overheard something in class. I began to suspect something was up when four juniors 'friended' me." She gave the quotation-marks gesture with an eye roll.

"Look." Brigita handed her a piece of paper that had been on the desk. "A letter came yesterday from the PTA. They're calling for a meeting, your transfer, an inquiry."

"They are out of their minds!" gasped Kristina.

"Of course they are," said Brigita. "But you know what this is like. We scramble and patch things together for years, and then something like this nonsense with the municipal signage comes along. You, as their teacher, shouldn't be making public comments about things. I mean, you're welcome to entertain whatever opinions you like—I don't care; we all have opinions. And besides, we all know who's been up to what around here. But do avoid clashing with students on Facebook. You'll make problems for yourself, and for all of us, and we don't need that."

"I see." She paused briefly, and then asked, "What are you going to do?"

"I'll do what I can to calm them down, for starters . . . and besides, what you wrote wasn't so bad."

"I didn't comment; all I wrote was—"

"I know; it was sent to me. 'The Thompson concert! Be there or be square! And if you don't come to the concert, watch Channel 3 at home.' I think the fuss is overblown, but best leave Thompson and his Croatian right-wing extremism out of our classrooms, especially in the context of your Serbian students. So they don't take what you said as a threat."

"A threat?" asked Kristina.

"Well, that's how the kids understood it, or so the letter claims."

"Oh, come on, please. Who's behind this? What threat? I'm their champion, and they know it . . . I can't believe this!" Kristina stuttered.

"I guess Mrs. Olivera Vujanović is running this particular show; she's writing the letters and is extremely active in protecting their Serbian *identity*, as she puts it—scandalized by discrimination and violent attempts to assimilate them into the Croatian community."

"Vujanović—ah, I should have known." Kristina pursed her lips and paled ever so slightly. "Did you see the cake she brought in for School Day?"

"No, I did not." This conversation was beginning to fray Brigita's nerves. Her thoughts were straying far from school and the problems with parents, professors, ethnicities, and singers, like Thompson and Ceca, who toyed with politics.

"The icing was decorated with the Serbian white eagle and the Only-Unity-Saves-the-Serbs symbol, and then she even posted a picture of the cake to Facebook, like she was saying,

This is how we celebrate our School Day, in this, our *city, with* our *Super Serbia cake.*"

"Fine. Let it go, please; that is the worst they can do. From now on, stay away from Facebook and comments. Leave this to me. Listen, I have to go; I have a meeting at two o'clock . . ." She was eager to wrap things up, but she noticed that though she was trying to calm her, Kristina seemed increasingly agitated. Her gaze wandered off, but then it fixed on the sheet of paper and the signature of Mrs. Vujanović, PTA president. A name known far and wide.

Olivera Vujanović owned several local butcher shops and was patroness of the Serbian saints' day celebrations, the self-appointed guardian of ethnic identity and the daughter of Predrag Vujanović—who was murdered. He had been one of the commanders of the territorial defense forces, a prominent city butcher before the war, whose refrigerator trucks in mid-autumn of 1991 were crammed, during the siege of the city, with dead Croatian bodies. According to testimony by the witnesses at the Belgrade trial, he'd been a particularly vicious executioner at the Velepromet warehouse and a close former collaborator of Stanko Velimirović, a man who was a city councilman today and leader of the Serbian opposition. Vujanović, Olivera's father, was one of the commanders of the Begejci camp, through which some five hundred Croatian prisoners passed in 1992, packed into stalls with concrete floors meant for livestock. A thin layer of straw for bedding.

Though this was not widely known, Olivera came to visit her father several times there, bringing with her in the trunk of her Yugo compact car—the car having been stolen for her from the army as a gift for her twenty-first birthday—a load of booze, cigarettes, ham, and smoked sausages from the attics of the houses Serbs had plundered. In the month after the siege was broken and the city fell to the Serbs, the territorial fighters were in particularly gleeful spirits almost every night, and around midnight they'd come barging into the barn, howling and forcing the Croatian prisoners to stand. In the corner of the barn stood a father in front of his seventeen-year-old son. The trembling shadows in the corners were always the most tantalizing for the guards. They sniffed out the stench of fear, discovered the fragile boy hidden behind his dad. *He's as cute as a girl; come on, old man, look at that ass; pretend he's your daughter.* Tears furrowed the man's face, and the boy's big brown eyes bugged out like wild chestnuts. Some puked; most had little but bile left to vomit. Some wet themselves. But one of them, Ante, fixed his eyes on a distant point. He was able to turn a blind eye to any crimes as long as he saved his own skin. If they'd only known, the skeletal wraiths around him would have throttled him, but they all thought he was being dragged off for questioning each time he was taken out by the guards. In fact, Ante was occasionally slipped a slice of sausage and a swig of brandy as his reward for informing on his fellow prisoners. He'd sit with the Serbian guards in the room while they played cards and drank. That night as well, they pulled him out and questioned him about who was cozying up to whom. The abuse had now acquired a new dimension, and he answered automatically, grateful for each new question. Olivera served the brandy and arranged the delicacies on a platter. Her careful arrangement of the smoked meats she'd sliced so artfully at an angle seemed pure madness in such a place. She kept sneaking glances at the prisoner while holding the slicing knife, and with a wry grin she went over to him. Knife in hand. He shut his eyes, gulping dried spittle with air, knowing the day would come when he'd pay for all the answers he'd given to the men who were asking. Then he felt the woman's moist lips on his. The red strawberry of her tongue. He didn't dare open his eyes. Silence in the room. He felt her hand slipping down between the elastic waistband of his tracksuit and his gaunt belly. She pulled out his dick and sat on it. He sobbed and moved his pelvis; she kissed his cheeks, knife in hand. "I like you," she whispered in his ear. Then he orgasmed and sank away. She laughed. She pulled up his tracksuit and turned the volume on the transistor back down. The Tiger fighters came back in. "Did you cut it off?" they howled. "There wasn't much," she quipped coyly. She came to him another three times, brought cigarettes, warm socks, underwear. Then her father, Predrag, had Ante exchanged, damn him, out of shame that his crazy daughter had the hots for an enemy fighter. The space around him and his warm socks in the barn was now empty. He missed her later and, later, he also wanted to kill her. Olivera spent the next year and a half at her aunt's in Mladenovac, in Serbia.

Then she returned to the city, single mother, by then, of Dejan Vujanović—later Kristina's student in the junior class of the high school where she taught—a tall, bright-eyed boy who sat near the back of the room. When he was assigned an open-ended essay, he wrote about the poems of Delimir Rešicki for his Croatian language class, and about Branko Miljković's poems for his Serbian class. A boy who mostly smoked by himself on the school grounds, absorbed in his music and poetry; he organized interviews for the school paper and drew wry comic strips. He listened attentively to Kristina in class and gave her that rare pleasure in teaching she'd found now and then among junior-year students, which made up for all the dimwits who were waiting only for the next soccer game so they could brawl. Little Dejo was Kristina's neighbor in her apartment building, and she still remembered him from when he was a child, when she and Ante first moved back to the city. He never made trouble. Once, long before, a few years back, she heard him through her open window when he was playing with the other children on the street, and she'd never forget it. He was about ten, living in a neighborhood where there were very few other Serbian kids, and he called out: "Whoever wants to be on my team, raise three fingers"—and then he added, in a singsong voice, "or two . . .". This moment of his sensitivity to the fact that Serbian kids responded by raising three fingers while Croatian kids raised two was something that would have been almost impossible to explain to anybody, especially anyone who wasn't from the city. Every so often his mother would pick on someone and harass them, and now Kristina's turn had come. And all because of that thoughtless comment she'd posted to Facebook about the Thompson concert. She wasn't even a fan; Thompson was no Bruce Springsteen, but Ante was the spokesperson for the veterans on the city council and he had tickets for VIP seats, so she was going. Though this seemed pointless to her, especially now, when one group was putting up signs in Serbian Cyrillic all over town and another group was tearing them down.

3.
Moving toward

they say
they don't recognize me

now (fall 2010)

Her first interviewee that morning lived on Švapsko Hill, along Republike Austrije Street. She hadn't made an appointment; it was more effective to show up unannounced. Despite everything being nearby, Nora hadn't made sense of what the receptionist-in-training explained to her on the map with its tangle of one-way streets. "Go straight, and at Kruna Mesara turn right," he said, but Nora was bad at following maps. She was never entirely sure where she was, where she was walking from, where she was going; in short, her position in her mind and her position on the outside did not necessarily coincide. She realized she could easily waste the entire morning, so off she went to the bus station, close by, hoping to find a cab. She spotted an Opel Corsa in a parking lot along the way, but when she got to the terminal, there were no cabs. Just as she'd made her peace with setting out on foot and stopping someone every so often to check if she was going in the direction of Kruna Mesara, the cab driver from the night before stepped out of a small store. Nora was the one, now, who walked up to him. He gave no sign that he'd ever seen her before. She stood in his path.

"Taxi?" she asked with a wary smile.

This threw him off. He looked at her, surprised, and then, as if only then recalling that he drove a cab, he said:

"I'm not driving just now, sorry; I'm busy, in something of a rush."

"But last night you were here. You offered me a ride, remember?" Nora wasn't backing down. She was surprised he didn't remember. What else was going on? The night before, he'd *really wanted* to be a cab driver. Nora didn't think of herself as a particularly memorable person, but she didn't expect to be so completely ignored. At thirty she could still pass as a student. She was one of those women who didn't stand out right away, with her midlength light hair tied back, usually, in a careless twist, always in slim jeans and dark tops. She was built like a boy, with a symmetrical face, an olive-hued complexion, and ever-so-slightly slanted eyes. But if a person looked at her more closely, her face was not easily forgotten. When she gave a heartfelt laugh, which was rare, she warmed up the room. When she listened closely to the person she was talking to, her eyes drinking in every gesture and the hue of the conversation, the person had to look away. Too intense. Perhaps because she seldom approached anything superficially, except the things she preferred to forget.

"Just one ride?" she pleaded.

"Okay, but where? As long as it's not too far . . ."

"Švapsko Hill, Republike Austrije Street, near the Kruna—"

"Mesara, I know; that's not ten minutes from here."

"I know, but as I'm not familiar . . ."

"Okay, off we go, but you'll have to make your way back on your own."

"No problem, I'm sure I'll manage."

The cab driver unlocked the doors. The inside of the old car was spotless. And she noticed there were no insignia hanging from the rearview mirror, or anywhere else on display—no rosaries, coats of arms, declaring allegiance to one side or the other. There were not even any stickers suggesting who the driver's favorite soccer team was, only a little green tree-shaped air freshener that gave off a penetrating scent of green apple. She hadn't seen a cassette player in a car for years; as they started off, the driver switched it on. There were speakers only in front, barely audible over the rumble of the motor, but despite all the noise she still recognized the voice of Johnny Štulić, and the words *tvoje ruke u neskladu*, "your hands in discord" . . . Music like this always sent her spinning back in time; those singers and beats were from a different era—song lyrics people seldom listened to anymore, yet the words said so much. About a time that was lived, a time now so far away that whatever was left of life was forever catching up. When they set off, she remembered there was another meeting to schedule, this one with Kristina's former principal, whom she'd called the night before. She'd been promised an interview today. The principal interested her because a recording had been made public a few weeks before of the mayor trying to bribe the woman, but, to Nora's regret, a colleague, not she, had been assigned that story.

Though she didn't ask him to, when she took her cell phone from her purse the cab driver turned the volume down without looking at her, and this gave her an instant to study his profile. He had a largish nose, attractive, sharp.

"Hello?" said the voice over the phone.

"Hello, forgive me, am I speaking to Ms. Arsovska?"

"Yes, who's this?"

"Nora Kirin here, from *Vrijeme*. I wrote to you last week. Calling about this afternoon? A half hour is all I need, a brief conversation . . . I know others have called you, but I won't be much of a bother. It's about Kristina, a teacher at your school . . ."

"Listen, I've said all there is to say about her, and I have a very full schedule. It's a tragic story; I regret that I have nothing to add."

"I won't mention you by name. But I do need to clarify a few points."

"You won't mention me by name? The media has been besieging me recently . . ."

"I won't, I promise; it's about Kristina."

"Okay, fine, but just half an hour. Hotel Lav; I'll get back to you about the time."

"Thank you. Looking forward."

She was glad to think she'd be done with her interviews by evening and would be able to catch the last bus for Zagreb, or the first one out the next morning, and get away from here.

"Thirteen?" The taxi slowed.

"Let me check." Nora glanced at her pad. "Yes, thirteen." She looked over at him. "How did you know? I didn't give you the number."

He pulled up in front of a small gray house, identical to all the other houses all down the block, the only difference being the house number. Once a city has been ravaged and leveled, nothing can bring it back to life. Even with vast effort, neighborhoods that used to have a special feel now looked more like an artificial arm or leg, a prosthetic limb of brick, concrete, and iron. He turned to her and said:

"I heard you were taking about Kristina, the teacher. This is a small city, and everyone knows everybody else. Ante's mother lives here, and I doubt she'll open the door for you. But, hey, go for it."

Nodding, Nora got out of the cab. Everything he was saying made sense.

"Thanks; still, I'll try." Just then she remembered she hadn't paid him, nor had he asked her for money, and she began rummaging through her purse.

"No problem," he said, "my meter's broken."

"Gee, really? Thanks . . ."

She stepped away from the car and walked toward the front gate. The Corsa turned, and then the driver rolled down the window.

"Nora!" He called her by name. "Take care."

This struck her as odd. He didn't give her the impression of being an overly courteous man, though she liked the quip about the meter; apparently he was observant.

She didn't see a doorbell by the door. There was a button to the right on the doorframe, but no name on it. She decided to try. When she pressed it, she heard the harsh buzz of the bell, and then, a half minute later, the shuffle of feet across the floor. From the dark belly of the front hall came a snow-white head, a foot or so below her eye level. The old woman looked up at Nora.

"Who are you?" she asked in a rasping voice, with no greeting.

"Forgive me for disturbing you." She hadn't been prepared for this. "I am a journalist, Nora Kirin; I would like to ask you a few questions, if you don't mind."

"What do you want? Don't come trampling on the dead bones of my Ante," the old woman said tartly, in lieu of an answer.

"Ma'am, I can't begin to imagine how this has been for you, but if you could spare me a few minutes, it would mean a lot to me." Her eyes drew even more to a slant. This was the moment when Nora really gazed into another person, trying to understand, and her gaze did, indeed, shake the old woman, but only for a moment.

"Leave me alone—what do you want to know? All I ever had has been slaughtered, burned, driven away, and now my beloved boy's been killed. Prison is not enough for that whore . . . I saw what a snake she was."

"Kristina?" She tried, with every ounce of her urgency, to keep the conversation going, at least in the doorway.

"I told him then, 'Why couldn't you find a normal woman, one of ours, who'd look after you, who'd bear you children! And not this teacher; did you need that?'"

"What do you mean, 'one of ours'?" The word "ours" immediately burned in Nora's ear; she knew what "ours" and "theirs" meant around here.

"*Ours!* That Chetnik bitch's father fled the city way back at the beginning, and she and her mother went around telling everyone the poor man was shot, who knows by whose bullet . . . Damned half-breed." The woman's eyes filled with tears, and her sparse, pure-white hair was swept by a draft at the open door. This information about Kristina's father's background was new to Nora, and she wasn't certain she could trust it. Just when she was about to ask for clarification, the old woman seemed to come out of a hypnotic trance and shot her a piercing look.

"Leave me alone, and don't you come back here again!"

Nora was still holding her breath, feeling the warmth wash over her through the doorway and rise to her ears, which were, by now, beet red. She stood for a few minutes at the slammed door before she breathed again, and then she turned, trying to remember which road the cab had come along to bring her there. The streets on Švapsko Hill were steep and zigzagging. The best idea was to go downhill, following the slope, and keep her fingers crossed that this would bring her to a place she'd recognize. The conversation hadn't given her much. The old woman, seared with fury and pain, had nothing left to hope for. Nora wondered how she spent her days alone in that house— how she woke up each morning and how she got up out of bed. It would be so much simpler to stay burrowed under the covers. And was there, when the old woman first opened her eyes, that moment when the memory of the horror hadn't hit her yet? That state of floating into consciousness that lasted maybe two or three seconds, when the body, brain, heart haven't yet adapted to reality, horror still hasn't etched itself in the body's DNA, and reality is only gradually settling? Nora could still summon that feeling at times. Every single day, at least one random event bolstered her conviction that her decision never to have children was the right one. Nobody won. Things were set up in such a way that something always happened, whether to the child or the parent. And after that, the remainder of one's life was reduced to memories, waiting, repeat.

Walking toward the center of town, Nora jotted down a few notes on her pad: *Chetnik bitch, children, Kristina's father.* On her way down the hill, she decided to find a place where she could order a decent meal. She'd skipped the hotel breakfast that morning and could no longer remember when she'd last had a proper dinner. Her next appointment was set for some yet-to-be determined time in the afternoon, at the Hotel Lav café.

She chose a table with a view over the Danube. She had her back to the entrance, so all she could see in front of her was the fat, murky green river, which she loved to watch flowing by. As a little girl, she'd been horrified by the sight of uprooted trees swept along in the currents. They traveled so slowly, but their shapes were still difficult to see clearly, changing in the watery mists. The branches jutting from the tree trunks reminded her of the arms of a drowning person waving to attract attention, but though they held their branching arms high the whole time, nobody seemed to notice. A hand appeared suddenly on the table next to her notebook, cell phone, and pens. A man's hand, with a gold signet ring on the little finger. The owner of the hand was standing over her, his other hand across the back of Nora's chair, watching her with tiny, watery blue eyes, a thin nose, and barely noticeable lips. His face looked as if it had been sketched by a six-year-old, with no color, details, or affect. When the straight lip line moved, he spoke—"The lovely lady is dining alone?"—and it spread into something like a smile. Nora turned, caught short by the question.

"Yes; I mean . . ."

"May I join you? I, too, am dining alone, and we could keep each other company," he wheedled, reminding her of one of the characters from the Topalović family and their funeral parlor in the cult film—what was it called? From the old days of ex-Yugoslavia. She thought she remembered the words "marathon" and "family" in the title, but wasn't sure. Yet this man seemed to be a character straight out of that film, right there in front of her, snapping his fingers to signal to the waiter that his place setting should be moved to her table.

"Godnar." He extended his hand, solemnly, across the table.

She wondered for a moment whether the name he'd given was his first name or surname, and then decided to respond:

"Nora," and shook his hand with a nod, and her hand was already at his lips. She quickly pulled it back, slipping it under the table.

"Godnar?" she asked. "An unusual name."

He concurred with a slight bow, and then explained.

"It's my artistic nom de plume, Grozdan Godnar."

"I see," she said, and struggled not to laugh.

"It comes from two words." After every sentence he gave a dramatic pause. "God, and Narcissus, and I'll only tell you my real name the second time we meet." She thought she saw him wink.

"Right," said Nora. "And what sort of art do you practice?"

"I am a poet," he declared, exalted.

"From around here?" she asked.

"Indeed. Although I haven't been living here for some time, so to speak. Tonight I'm presenting a volume of my poems, dedicated to my native city, so if you aren't busy elsewhere, I will be so bold as to invite you to my reading from *Elegy for a City*. You look like a poetry lover." After the remark, founded on nothing, he fished a book out of his briefcase. The cover design was remarkably ugly: his face. When he showed her the foreword, written by Peter Handke, things fell into place for Nora, though she was no poetry aficionado. She remembered that Handke was known as an outspoken supporter of Serbs, so this Godnar fellow must be a member of the city's expatriate Serbian community. During their aimless and even bizarre conversation, she did whatever she could to steer him toward what was currently going on in the city, but this soon proved nearly impossible, as the poet spoke of nothing but himself and his *philosophical* take on the world. He treated her to a few lines of verse from his collection in which celestial motifs followed one after another; the *patriarch as glorious transgressor, alchemy as the cross* and the poetic subject who *was crucified every day in the labyrinthine circle* . . . Before the end of lunch, when she asked him whether he'd heard of the case of the teenage lover, the schoolteacher, and her murdered husband, he presented his theory:

"Ah, all the murders . . . you know . . ." He shook his head with resignation. "Our entire population lives, flounders, and dies in their grim Slavic legacy. And when the passions of love light up this little life, it must drown here in blood! And then everyone wants to know: Who's to blame? Who's to blame? But they don't realize that a night of spectral will has descended upon them . . . Why, those very words appear in the title of one of my poems, one of the finer ones, actually. This city experienced the fate of a lost lamb facing a horde of ravenous wolves . . . And that, too, arises in my poems."

"Ah, yes," was all that Nora had to add to the man's lyric excess, glancing at her watch. "Sorry, but I must get going; I have a meeting." She tried to bring the lunch to an end while checking her cell phone, just as a text message flashed on the screen from Brigita Arsovska: *I won't be able to make it today . . . Tomorrow at the earliest. Greetings.*

"One more thing I must tell you . . . You probably wondered whether this was pure happenstance that I came and sat at your table. It was not. You know, today is my wedding anniversary, and you remind me irresistibly of my wife—in her younger years, of course."

"Please convey my warm regards to your wife," she replied as she stood up from the table. She needed fresh air, exercise; she had accomplished almost nothing.

4.

Years of lead

a thousand years
open the door
unbuckle me

before (spring 2010)

"Scat, scat, children, Satan's coming!" hollered Granny Anđa, shooing the children off the road and into the front yard. Never before had she seen a man with dark skin, though her Herzegovina relatives working in Germany, when they came back for the holidays, told of all sorts of men, and women, too, who walked freely about the streets, dark- or sallow-skinned, tattooed, alone or in couples, black and white together. Josip crouched by the wrought-iron gate, hiding behind his granny's skirts, and when Satan himself, in a hat and long leather coat, walked by their house, Josip darted out and threw a stone at him, striking the man in the ankle. His granny shouted, "You little devil, Josip, git ye back in here!" and the dust-smeared children who had run up from the depths of the yard hollered: "Yaaaaa!"

Satan turned only once, already inured to slights during his brief stay in the Vojvodina village in northern Serbia, and looked with sadness into the eyes of the little boy who'd cast the stone. The child glared back at him, unblinking, defiant, and in the boy's eyes there was nothing but an unchecked desire for destruction. Josip Ilinčić had been brought to Plavna, Vojvodina, on a special resettlement train when he was but a tiny bundle, in the company of his granny Anđa and his mother, Iva, only ten years after the end of World War II. His father stayed to work in Germany, and as soon as Josip finished eighth grade he was sent off to a seminary in Herzegovina, where his uncle lived. He was the middle child of a brood of five, bright and with no strong bonds to anyone, cold, incisive, with a future as a friar. One summer when he was just over eighteen, about to make his commitment to the life that had been chosen for him, he came home to visit his mother, grandmother, and younger sisters. At a village church fair he caught sight of Mariška, all flashing black eyes and pink cheeks. At night—after breathing in her boots, after gazing at her tanned neck and string of golden beads, after burning up with fever by the open window, his eyes stinging and his whole body aching—he made up his mind to approach her. Gaunt, tall, never one to crack a smile, he floundered when he found himself in the proximity of her free-flowing sensuality. The snub was not the worst thing that had ever happened to him, but he never forgot her teasing giggles and the jeers of the older boys and girls around her. They yelled *Reverend* and *Hail Mary* after him, while he, with measured steps, strode away from the lewd jibes that tore at his ears. When night fell, he waited for the darkest moment before dawn and went to Mariška's house. From the street below he heaved in a flaming rock wrapped in gasoline-soaked gauze. When the first hungry flames licked the wooden beams, he strode back home with measured step. He did not return to the seminary; with the help of a friend of his uncle's he enrolled in the school of law in Osijek.

The outbreak of war found him there. He was mustering resources to start a new movement for Croatia, sizzling with excitement at the very thought of all the weapons that would be rattling around him. His heart pounded faster at the sounds of the distant detonations approaching; the external state of incipient chaos was finally in sync with his inner self, understood by no one. He sniffed out the right people for the changes to come. Up onto the stage he clambered, sputtered all over the microphone, pumped his fist in the air. Every time someone said *sir* in a God-fearing voice, he knew for a certainty that they must be speaking to him. The most auspicious turn of events for him and his boys was when their country, which—as they'd announced to everyone—they were building anew, came under assault. This was perfect timing: he and his boys were compelled to rally to the country's defense. Their reputation as defenders of the homeland was their only sliver of superiority over the crimes the other side was perpetrating, and for a few years they were lauded as heroes. When the collective madness began, the puzzle was a simple one to solve for the shrewder minds among them. What they required was a climate of fear, the flood of media articles on the attacks, the Chetniks, *the enemies in our midst*, and if the enemy failed to provide the fodder they needed, they'd cook up more discord themselves. The critical voices could be silenced readily enough using blackmail and threats; exceptions were rare. Special Police Officer Kirin, who had been dispatched to the negotiations, began raising his voice against the acts deliberately designed to incite strife, the attacks on Serbian civilians, the Croatian guns trained on Croatian villages. The more Ilinčić and his boys strove to persuade Kirin that this behavior was not serving *our* cause, the more intransigent Kirin became, until he was burned to death one day in a "car crash," his car ablaze as it plunged off a bridge. Never was the man identified who'd driven the car that forced Kirin's off the road; the police were too busy just then pursuing *real* criminals. The "car crash" gave Ilinčić and his boys the elbow room they wanted. Surviving Kirin's death were his widow and twelve-year-old daughter. They were given well-meaning advice to accept the condolences, the flag, the medal, and then, at least for a time, clear out of Osijek. Everything else went smoothly, according to plan. By then so many people had been killed in the fighting that Josip and his boys were beginning to look like true-blue champions of the people. What would be the upside, anyway, of trumpeting the news to all and sundry that the battles, the bloodshed, and the sacrifice of an entire city had been concocted underground, in cahoots with the enemy? The ordinary people would never have understood how wars are really won anyway. Each of the two warring sides was led by a player of equal prowess. Ilinčić led one of the sides. At his behest the sun rose and set in Eastern Slavonia, and at his side every step of the way was a young man by the name of Schweppes, a bodyguard at the time, only nineteen, a murderer and criminal who'd come of age in the gambling establishments of the capital city. Schweppes was quick, agile, and invisible. Trailing behind him was a whole string of unsolved crimes, including an elegant car crash when, fancying himself the Hollywood tough guy and propelled by white-powder brashness, he forced the target and the target's car into a ravine. Schweppes shadowed Ilinčić's every step.

The other side was led by Stanko Velimirović. In November 1991, the esteemed Dr. Velimirović set aside everything else in his life to stand before the cameras of the international television crews, determined to bring down the *last bastion of the Ustashas*: the general hospital, crowded with civilians and the wounded. Under his watchful eye, drunken paramilitaries did what they did as if sober: they murdered the wounded, dumped the bodies in gaping pits in the ground, and raped all the women who'd stayed in the city. Shadowing Velimirović's every step was a young man named Marko. Marko was an eighteen-year-old reservist, the sharpest sniper of his generation, loyal, silent, smart. Recruited from the rank and file of Yugoslav People's Army regulars, he was a boy with no father, living with his ailing mother. Velimirović trusted Marko completely and commanded him—during the night the Serbs broke the seige and took control of the city—to organize security units for one of the mass graves, the pit. The next night, Marko showed up before dawn in Velimirović's bedroom. He made the man's wife kneel on the floor, bound her hands, duct-taped her face; Velimirović woke only when he felt a pistol muzzle thrust between his teeth, then a blow to the temple. He couldn't see in the dark; all he could hear was a hoarse whisper—Marko's.

"Don't you ever come looking for me again. For you, I'm dead. If you try, I have all the evidence; are you listening? The locations, the photographs, everything you've done; stored in a safe place. As you know, these times will, one day, be behind us. I've protected myself, and if anything happens to me or my mother, you're done for." Then he shoved the pistol muzzle once more against the roof of Velimirović's mouth and, without a sound, left as he'd come. Velimirović didn't fear violence, but he did fear a sharp mind, and he had no doubts about Marko's. After that night, he pretended the two were strangers, though both of them went on living in the city and crossed paths now and then. When the Croats began moving back to the city during the peaceful reintegration, Velimirović stepped into the role of leader of the Serbian side. He was complicit enough in war crimes that his electorate trusted he wouldn't be able to turn his back on their complicity. He was also eloquent enough to stand in front of TV cameras and on the city council.

Since the end of the war there'd been no moment as lucrative as this: the kerfuffle over the installation of signs throughout the city in the Serbian Cyrillic alphabet and the enraged response of local Croats, who defiantly tore down the Cyrillic signage.

The story behind the signs was a simple one. The law requiring that signs be installed on all municipal buildings in both the Croatian and Serbian alphabets had been passed some ten years after the return of the Croats to the city, at a moment when the government was being run by the right-wing Croatian political party. The party leader was an obsequious bureaucrat, while almighty Josip Ilinčić hunkered, powerful, in the shadows. When city hall began to roil with corruption scandals, evaporating renovation funds, wholesale nepotism, it became clear that the local government was about to lose the next election to more liberal Croatian parties. This was when the right wing devised a cunning plan: they'd create a coalition of their party and the party of the Serbian ethnic minority, whose ranks still included veterans from wartime paramilitaries. In exchange for joining this coalition, the Serbs demanded concessions, and the Croatian right wing was in no position to refuse. One of the concessions was that if the day should come when the number of Serbs living in the city were to top 33 percent of the population, Cyrillic signs would be installed on all the municipal buildings. This gave Serbian voters the impression that they'd won an important battle, while the Croatian right wing had no intention of ever actually following through.

Neither of the brilliant coalition partners anticipated, of course, that the day would ever dawn when they'd have to implement the law. When it did come, and when, again, demonstrations erupted, Velimirović and Ilinčić found ways to profit. The entire city was seething, and the mayor wasn't handling any of this well, distracted as he was by having to buy support for his upcoming mandate.

The social unrest in the city turned out to be manna from heaven. The national government was searching for ways to distract attention from a third year of recession, so they spiced things up with the time-tested formula of inciting interethnic strife. Every morning when he scanned his newspapers and portals, Velimirović rubbed his hands with glee at the multitude of political manipulations that were suddenly possible. When he and Ilinčić bumped into each other in the corridors of city hall during those days, their nods to each were like silent high fives. After so many people had been killed in and around the city, stoking the situation to the white heat of conflict would be a breeze, wouldn't it? The most recent flash point Velimirović knew of was the trouble facing the Croatian-language teacher who'd supposedly threatened schoolchildren on Facebook. This reminded him to call his media expert, a promising young reporter at *Izbor*, the local periodical for the Serbian ethnic minority, funded by the national budget but run directly from Velimirović's desk.

"So, Nikola, how goes it?"

"Brilliant, Boss, I'm working on the new issue; we go into layout tomorrow. And how's by you?"

"Splendid, Nikola, splendid! Thanks for asking . . . Any updates on that teacher?"

"Teacher? Oh, the one with the Facebook scandal? Sure, a few words, but to tell you the truth, I don't see much there."

"Nikola, my boy, if you write a strong text, something will surface. Get my drift?"

"Sure. You think I should?"

"I do."

"Fine, I'll have a look."

"There you go, my boy; we don't want our children being victimized in their classrooms," chuckled Velimirović, and Nikola got the drift. The last text to be laid out the next day had as its headline: "The Street Spills Over into the Classroom."

$$ \text{\small ❧ \qquad ❧ \qquad ❧} $$

We're sinking
I'm not here
not there not here

This beggared belief. If only there were a way for her to wake up from this nightmare. It was morning, and Kristina was curled up in bed on her side, wide awake, her eyes closed, listening to

Ante getting ready to leave. Recently he was going off to meetings bright and early: first a stop at the local bar, then to a shift spent guarding the municipal offices against the Cyrllic signs, then to the Veterans' Association offices, then back to the bar, and then someone would roll him home in the dead of night. The night before last he was delivered in an ambulance; they carried him, only barely conscious, to his bed. First he'd drunk himself into a stupor and engaged in a fistfight with a policeman, and he ended up at the psychiatric ward. With him in the ambulance was Svetlana, a nurse, who worked on the ward and was also a neighbor in their apartment building. Although she was a Serb, Ante respected her; he'd grown accustomed to her and the homemade doughnuts she sometimes brought them. After they settled him in, Kristina and Svetlana went out onto the balcony for a smoke. His behavior was no longer embarrassing for Kristina. The hospital—in a city where, fifteen years earlier, some five thousand people had been killed—didn't have a single psychologist on staff, though every home in the city had at least one family member suffering from PTSD. And PTSD, like every disease, did not afflict only the more upstanding members of society. Perhaps PTSD made the good people better and the bad people worse. After all her years of marriage, Kristina was clear about which category her husband belonged in. She didn't even make the effort to ask Svetlana for the details; Svetlana jumped in to tell her without being asked.

"I'm standing there by the reception desk when I hear a man caterwauling: he'll fuck their mothers, slit their throats, the shits . . . you know the routine . . ." Here she stopped.

"Oh, I do," answered Kristina, wanting to spare both of them the repetition.

"And only then did I see it was him. He wouldn't even let them help him walk, and he couldn't walk, he kept jerking free. And then he saw me and suddenly stopped in his tracks, went all quiet, looked over at me, and said, 'Gee, Ceca, sorry; I didn't mean you.'"

"What an asshole," said Kristina through clenched teeth.

"I didn't know whether to laugh or cry," said Svetlana.

"Next time they should just leave him out on the street." Kristina snorted.

"Well, what can you do . . . This trouble is bad. What the hell are they after with the signs and the Cyrillic; they're driving people crazy. Who the fuck cares which alphabet they use on my pink slip."

"Thanks, Svetlana." Kristina was tired and needed time to herself. She'd had it. The harassment at school, Ante's shenanigans—the insults and the drinking. She glanced from the balcony into the gloom of the apartment where his body lay sprawled out on the bed. She wished he'd never move again. That was two nights ago. As of yesterday, she'd called in sick. Because of the troubles at school. Now she was in bed, feigning sleep, hoping he'd leave her in peace and quiet. Maybe everything would be different if they'd had kids, but they didn't. Maybe it would have been different if her father's grave were out there somewhere, but it wasn't. He had left at the very start of the war and never came back. Kristina was mature enough to understand that her parents didn't love each other, and somewhere deep inside her she knew this was the real reason he left. The fact that his leaving just so happened to coincide with the outbreak of war, that he was a Serb, that she and her mother ended up in refugee accommodations in a tourist hotel on the

Adriatic coast, that he was pronounced dead and later rumors reached them that he'd been seen in Belgrade—these things were nobody's fault, least of all hers. Maybe things between her and Ante would have been at least a little different if there hadn't been all those people talking behind his back, ignoring his war medals, whispering about what went on while he was an internee at the prison camp. Everything had come to a head, and life with him was unbearable. The only thing Kristina enjoyed was her job, her escape valve, and now that, too, was crumbling. She noticed Ante had begun tormenting her less; he seemed almost approving of the troubles she was having at school after what she'd written on Facebook. But nothing she did could ever fully convince him she could be trusted.

She didn't have the strength to get up out of bed, not even after he'd slammed the door, not even after he came back and rang the doorbell loud and long. Must have forgotten something. After he buzzed the third time she finally pulled on her bathrobe and shouted:

"Here! Coming!"

She unlocked the door without checking through the peephole first to see who was out there, and then she was astonished. It was Dejan standing in the doorway. Fumbling, head bowed, backpack on back, he said, softly:

"Hey there . . ."

"Dejan, what are you doing here? Why aren't you in school?" She could make no sense of this.

"I came to see how you're doing." He stared at the floor.

"Well, don't stand out there, come in." She took him into the dining room and pulled a chair out for him to sit at the table.

"I'll be with you in a minute; have a seat." Then she went into the bathroom and swiftly grabbed jeans and a T-shirt from the laundry basket. She tied her hair back in a ponytail, bent over the sink, and splashed her face with cold water. She glanced quickly at herself in the mirror, at her puffy eyes and a few lines on her face from her pillow. When she returned to the dining room, he was still hunched over in the chair, his schoolbag on his lap.

"Who'll write the note excusing your absence today? You shouldn't have come," she sighed and turned towards the kitchen, taking her coffee pot out of the cupboard.

"I'm so sorry about this mess," he said softly. Dejan knew that his mother, who was active on social media, was behind the attack on Kristina. She was relentless in her pursuit of Croats she saw as her enemies, always with the same fervor, seeking them near and far, but until now she hadn't stooped this low.

"Not your fault," said Kristina, her back turned. This child in her kitchen was no longer a child. He was on the verge of manhood, and he understood everything. She wondered how it was that he was so mature, considering where he was from, though in her thirty-four years, she'd gradually come to see that people are sometimes simply people. No matter which wringer you put them through. And he'd been exposed to good things, too, especially books. He'd already come to see her a few times to talk about what he was reading, though his mother and Kristina's husband knew nothing of his visits. He wasn't pushy, just determined, the way smart people sometimes are. He wanted to know, to read, to understand. Their conversations ranged across all sorts of things, bridging the age gap, the ghettos they each lived in, going beyond their formal relationship. As Dejan matured, the way he looked at her changed; his eyes dropped more often and the tenor of his voice shifted when he spoke. No one had looked at Kristina that way for a long time, and Ante probably never. In the last few years she had begun to feel in class that she was lecturing only to Dejan, adapting the teaching to what she thought would interest him. And now here he was, drenched in sweat, with a lump in his throat.

"I told her not to." He gazed straight at Kristina, open and vulnerable. She came over and sat down next to him.

"Don't let yourself be dragged into this; it will sort itself out." Though she didn't know how.

"She is not in her right mind. I want to move out; she'll be the death of me."

"Don't say that—where would you go? One more year and you'll enroll at university somewhere. As far away as possible. Until then, patience, for a little longer."

"But I don't want to leave here." There was nothing he was more certain of.

"Can't you see how people live here? Come on, please; you deserve better."

"I'm not going anywhere," he repeated, and then he added, "I won't leave you. I know what you go through . . . with him."

"Dejan." She smiled gently. "This will pass; everything does . . . and who knows, maybe I, too, will leave here one day."

"Fine, then that's when I'll go." His eyes burned as he spoke. He was wishing he could die, hug her; he only feared bursting into tears. They looked at each other for a long second, and then he shifted out of his own body and drew his chair over to hers. He took her hand in his moist hands and suddenly, almost tipping over his chair, kissed her squarely on the mouth, without parting his lips. Kristina didn't move. Then she took his hands, gently set them down, and pulled back.

"Dejan . . ." She had a shred of composure left and hesitated between clinging to it and letting go. He slid down off the chair, knelt at her feet, dropped his head into her lap. She didn't push him away this time; under her hands she felt him trembling, his shallow breaths. The next moment they were trembling together on the kitchen floor. A half hour later, when she handed him his backpack in the hallway, he pushed her up against the wall and kissed her for a long time. He still hadn't reined in the chaos churning inside him, so she smiled and said:

"You'll make it to third period."

He shot her a glance with so much seventeen-year-old adoration in it that for a long time afterward she remembered nothing but that she was alive.

It was nearly noon when the phone rang. Their cups of coffee were still on the table, and Kristina was lying on the sofa, channel surfing. She turned down the volume and stared for a time at the unfamiliar phone number on her cell phone screen. She clicked on it.

"Hello, may I please speak to Kristina Gelo," said a man's confident voice.

"Speaking, and this is . . . ?"

"Kristina, my dear, this is Josip Ilinčić; we've met before! I am on the city council and a friend of your husband's . . ."

"Ah, yes; how may I help you?" She was unsettled by his call and wanted him to get to the point as quickly as possible. He was a real snake in the grass; she could only guess why he'd called.

"Listen, I've been following what's been going on with you,

how you're being . . . hounded, am I right?" She could hear the hint of a sneer.

"Well, I hope the inquiry will establish that everything is fine and this will die down."

"Kristina, your actions are deserving only of praise, but let's not be naïve—they'll pulverize you." He sounded malicious and ominous. She couldn't be certain of what he had in mind, but she was alarmed.

"What can they do to me?"

"I don't want to scare you, please don't think I want that; everything will, chances are, quiet down, as you say. It's just that I think you should have a word with an attorney, you know, just in case." His offer wasn't entirely farfetched. After a pause, he went on, "And I'm here for you, because I want to help, see . . . *pro bono*, goes without saying. Why not get together for coffee, Kristina?"

She said nothing. The thought of having anything to do with the man was distasteful; she found him and his world revolting. She couldn't believe how far this had gone, and she went numb with fear.

"Fine, an hour from now, at Golubica."

"I'll be there. And don't you worry about a thing; we'll show them what's what."

She couldn't bear listening to him anymore and wasn't sure what to do. Passing by the muted TV, she saw the city, again, on the national news at noon. Again they were running the footage they'd filmed two days before as the backdrop to what the announcer was saying. A twenty-year-old woman with the same name, Kristina, had been anointed the heroine of the right wing. She stood on the city's main square, at attention, a black beret on her head, a sledgehammer in hand. In front of her was a wooden box, and on it were words written in Cyrllic: "aggressor," "treason," and more in the same vein. The heroine began swinging, splintering the box, the letters, smashing them. Chunks of wood, splinters, sprayed through the air, and bald, muscular men soon joined in on the act of vandalism, kicking the box. The artistic performance looked like a scene from hell. All that mattered was to break, smash, trample as violently as possible. After they'd obliterated the box, the heroine reached into the rubble and retrieved a clay pigeon wrapped in barbed wire. A crowd that had gathered applauded. Kristina dashed into the bathroom and vomited.

5.

Be alone on the street

*and I need a room
that will hold five thousand
with glasses raised,
glasses raised*

now (fall 2010)

Nora walked out of the hotel, leaving behind the elegiac poet and the book he'd been foisting on her, which she left on the seat of the chair next to hers, tucked under the thick folds of the tablecloth. It was early afternoon, and she decided to stroll through the city—ghostly empty at this hour, abandoned, as if everyone who could go had already left; the city had had no mayor for several weeks now. The high school principal, Brigita Arsovska, out of an overabundance of concern for the public good and her profound belief in the mission of the city council, had provided the media with a recording a few weeks before, during the summer break, in which the mayor could be heard attempting to buy her vote. Urging her to swerve from the right side of the aisle to the left to guarantee the passage of the municipal budget, to give him four more years of his mandate, which would mean the privatization of the port and the stretch of land in the duty-free zone that the mayor was treating as if it were his own backyard. At a pivotal moment Brigita felt he was getting much too much in return for her cooperation, while she would have to make do with nothing but a seat on an advisory board and the occasional excursion to Brussels. She was probably also worried that the leadership of her own party and cohort would retaliate, and she was learning just how rotten politics were, how bribery and corruption were rampant on all sides, and she felt compelled to expose the widespread hypocrisy to the community at large. Not long after she publicized the recording, once its authenticity had been verified, both of them were stripped of their functions. The mayor was soon replaced, and she was named as her own acting principal. Inspectors were sent to the school—this much the mayor was still able to pull off with the support system he'd rigged and the incident of the unhinged teacher—and the inspection was slated to include an in-depth examination of her work. The inspectors arrived to investigate, observed a number of irregularities in the work of the principal and the way she'd risen to her position. Brigita was not particularly concerned; she knew that soon *she would be in power*. Her only worries were the occasional late-night telephone calls from the almost ousted mayor that had been going on for weeks. He, clearly, was not prepared to give up so easily, especially not like this. He insisted they get together, and she was determined to avoid meeting with him. Everyone is running from someone, or from their own past.

Nora headed off toward the arcades and spotted several

bilingual signs on some buildings. This time they'd been mounted several feet above the standard height for signs and were fenced off with iron-mesh barriers. Not one of the rare passersby, most of them elderly, looked at the signs; as they walked they kept their gaze trained on the ground. A small, stooped woman hobbled by several feet in front of her, leaning on a cane. The coat she wore was so old-fashioned that it could almost have been fashionable, and she carried a small clutch purse. One more detail caught Nora's eye: the hand holding the purse was clad in a beige lace glove. She had nothing better to do, and she was dreading the prospect of interviewing Kristina's neighbors—statements from people like them were, to her mind, the dregs—so she turned to follow the woman. Just for a few minutes, a stroll. The woman turned toward the bridges at the confluence of the Vuka and the Danube, stopping every so often and gazing out over the wall into the water. She stopped by the back of Hotel Danube, looked across the river, and sat on the nearest bench. While Nora was passing her, they made eye contact. The old woman measured her and then, at the very last moment, said, in a raspy voice:

"Hello there."

"Hi!" responded Nora readily, remembering that people still conversed with strangers in the smaller cities and towns. "Cold?" she asked the old woman.

"Oh, no, I'm used to this. It turns nasty only when the wind blows."

"Yes, along the river the wind is different," added Nora, still torn between continuing her wander and her desire to talk.

"Like a seat?" The old woman made room for her on the bench.

"Sure, thanks."

"There aren't as many young people in the city as there used to be. The evening promenade was teeming. You couldn't even make your way across the bridge. The boys would stand to one side"—she waved to where the two rivers joined—"and up and down we'd parade, maybe ten times." She laughed, her lips dry.

"Are you from here?"

"From there!" Her hand was still midair, but she flipped it so it pointed toward the Hotel Lav. "But now I'm in a studio apartment. Which they gave me."

"They didn't rebuild your house?" asked Nora.

"Ugh," sighed the woman. "Rebuilt it and then took it."

"Took it?"

"My late uncle, Viktor Schwartz, when he died, why the whole city came out for the funeral, they all wept, young and old."

"You're from the Schwartz family?"

"I am Melania Gmaz." She nodded with dignity. "My mother, Hedvig, married into the Kirbaums, and my uncle ran a pharmacy, the finest one in the area. Jozefina Vraga worked there, and she's still alive; she's one hundred and six, you can ask her anything. She used to crochet the most exquisite pieces, and the ones I managed to save I gave to the museum." Melania nodded, descending momentarily into the past, and then rising back to the present, next to Nora on the bench.

"And who took your house?"

"My uncle, the late Viktor Schwartz, had no children, so I was sole heir. Once the war was over, the government renovated the pharmacy as a monument and then took it." She stopped for a moment and gave Nora a penetrating glance. "Do you, by any chance, work in television?"

"No, no . . . elsewhere."

"Well, I called them to come and have a look. At home I have five boxes of fully indexed papers. I used to work, you know, as an archivist, and I've kept everything in tip-top shape, but nobody's willing to show up, nobody cares. Now they've moved into the building and are playing dumb, as if it's already theirs. The fellow—you know, what's his name, the one who peels potatoes?" Nora caught on slowly. The former agriculture minister, a high-ranking politician, was one of the people convicted of fraud for millions of kunas for selling state-owned lands; he wasn't sentenced to prison time but to community service. Photographs had been flooding the media of him, as one of those making amends, as he peeled potatoes in a soup kitchen. His political party had apparently been using the home of Viktor Schwartz and Melania Gmaz as their headquarters. The building was a baroque edifice in the center of the city, which, according to famous Serbian and previously Yugoslav writers such as Momo Kapor, was nothing but a provincial, countrified copy of a baroque building, tantamount to an architectural slap in the face. The great Croatian patriots, however, saw it as war booty and moved their corrupt party right in, while for Melania the building had been her childhood home. No matter which of these stories Nora dug into, she found evidence of crimes, pits that could be covered over only by institutional lies.

"And I have another house—or, I should say, half a house." Melania smiled gently. "It is up on Priljevo, near the port. They offered me a thousand deutsch marks for it—sorry, damn it, euros."

"Who offered?"

"The people from the city, who else. They said, 'Grandma,

that's the most you'll ever get for it.' Well, screw you! I showed them a thing or two. I couldn't care less what happens once I up and die, but while I'm alive and kicking they will not get their grubby little hands on it." Her eyes filled with tears, and on she went: "I saw them the other day hanging around my house with that Chinese fellow; there's big money at play . . . They drove up in this big black car, and when the Chinese fellow left they were there in the parking lot. The mayor nearly came to blows with the man who has his fingers in every pie. Who knows what this is about? I wanted to call the police when I saw how he was picking the other guy up by the collar, but then they left."

"You're certain it was the mayor?" Nora wasn't entirely convinced by the story about the dustup in the parking lot.

"You bet I am. . . . The other man—the one who runs the hotel; you know who I mean—lifted Mr. Mayor up and threw him against a car. What animals! He's the one who actually runs the city anyway . . ." she added bitterly. "And then they stopped, so I didn't call it in." She fell silent, and after a pause, added:

"But they're not getting their claws on my house. As long as I'm still present and accounted for."

"Good for you," was all Nora could add. Melania pursed her lips and said nothing for a long stretch. She smoothed the lace on her glove, her eyes fixed somewhere deep in front of her. Nora, also, was quiet. She had no clear plans for the rest of the day. She could feel the city seething beneath the surface; why, only that morning she'd been thinking she'd be able to wrap up her assignment by nightfall, might write a few pages at the hotel and sign off on most of the story about the dragon lady. The article would be built on guesswork, packaged as presentable only thanks to the tools of the trade, and that was what was most repugnant to her. All she'd accomplished up to that point was a stuttering exchange with Ante's mother in the doorway to her house, a meeting with the former high school principal which had been put off to the next day, a weird invitation to an evening of poetry by a poet who penned elegiac verse about a city that had been smashed and murdered while he worked on advancing his international career. Still, she might run into interesting people at the poetry reading; it was worth going purely for curiosity's sake. On the other hand, she could always pick up a bottle of wine and spend the evening at the hotel, listening to reverberations from the deep inner life of the walls.

"You are so young, yet so pensive." Melania's voice interrupted her. "When I was your age I was leaping over buildings in a single bound, but that was a different time; everything has been lost . . . There's no more joy . . ."

"Gotta go," said Nora, feeling restless.

"Off you go, dear; don't let me keep you. It was a pleasure." Melania looked at her gently as Nora stood. She had already begun to walk away when she heard the voice behind her: "And go somewhere where there's sunlight and sea! Get away from this hole!"

Nora did not turn around.

⚜   ⚜   ⚜

Like it used to be
we trade our night
for someone else's day

The doorknob to the room dated back to the hotel's original inventory, brass and round. The door was opened by pressing the button in the middle of the knob. Halfway it went smoothly, and then jammed and took coaxing and jiggling to find just the right balance and open the door. There were two narrow beds in the room, and Nora, fully dressed, her shoes still on, flopped onto the one farther from the door. She lay on her side and stared at the other trimly made cot with its taut sheets. Then she stretched, reached out, and grabbed the pillow and pulled it to her, hugged it and plunged her nose into it. It had no smell at all, spongy, soft, impersonal hotel bedding. Outdoors, the evening was already settling, earlier and earlier these days, and the only sound coming through the wooden window frame was the beating of the wind and sloshing of waves on the broken remnants of a tugboat. The longer she lay in the condensing gloom that filled the room, the more difficult it would be, she knew, to get up and go out again. She lifted her head and switched on the little bedside lamp, but its wan yellow light only made the room feel more airless. She pulled her laptop from her backpack, opened it, and then remembered there was only Wi-Fi in the lobby and the restaurant. She typed a few notes to herself in an open document and then decided to go down to check her email. The hallways of the hotel were filled with a creepy silence; only when she'd moved deeper into the restaurant did she recognize the song coming from the dusty speakers as an Oliver Dragojević evergreen, with him singing, as ever, about boats and the sea. "I swear you look just like Oliver Dragojević," her mother had told a man who actually was Oliver Dragojević, as her father was so fond of telling their friends while Nora's mother blushed. And that happened right here, in the late eighties, while parties and concerts were still held on these premises, before the hotel became the headquarters for the new Serbian Krajina government. Nora's mother was a big fan of Oliver's, and her father decided to surprise her that night with tickets for his concert, to be held in the city's big sports arena. They went to Hotel Danube for dinner before the concert, and while they were greeting friends, a man sat at the table next to theirs. Nora's mother couldn't take her eyes off him or contain her surprise, and when she saw he'd noticed her, she told him, "I swear you look just like Oliver Dragojević." The man began to chuckle, along with the others at his table, and Nora's father whispered to her that the man was, indeed, Oliver Dragojević. At the time she wanted to curl up and die, but later she always enjoyed hearing her husband tell the story. They'd had a wonderful evening, and there was nothing whatsoever to lead them to think that within two or three years' time that whole life would be gone forever. Nora still enjoyed listening to her father in her thoughts, though the sound of his voice had grown quieter over the years, and the contours of his face were fading for her. Her memories had dwindled to flashes; his big hands, the image of which was still unusually sharp, the shape of his fingernails, the gray shocks of hair at his temples, fishing by the river, his gentle air of patience, rolling down the windows of their red Škoda, a hand raised in greeting. That was the last one. After that she saw his picture on television, the car wreck, the black body bag. The rest of what happened over those days she could only barely remember. Hardly anybody came to see them; there were only the occasional calls late at night that she was terrified to ask about and after which her mother retreated to the bathroom. And then came the real war, which became more and more real like a grimy cloud of dust, blanketing everything. Packing at night, a long trip on a bus, the fragrance of the sea. She allowed the sea fragrance to fill every hole in her memory; she gave up on her Slavonian accent and calling her friends "buds" and chose to tell everyone, instead, that she was from Omiš, so much closer to the coast than her real hometown but—like her hometown—a place refugees were streaming from. She became a Hajduk soccer fan, swam in the sea from May to October; soon she fit right in among the lithe, suntanned Dalmatians and, somehow, survived. Later she attended the university in Zagreb, where life was more bearable, and there she didn't have to make any special efforts to fit in. Nora from Omiš who goes *down to Dalmatia* to see her mother. At first, when they'd only just come "down to Dalmatia," her mother did whatever she could; she even went to the police a few times, hoping against hope that maybe the police stations in different parts of the country weren't all linked. The inspector—who, the first time around, listened to her story with surprise and interest about how she'd had suspicions that her husband was killed by *our side* because he went up against them about the war, because he spoke publicly about the crimes happening in Osijek—pretended he'd never seen her before when he ran into her two days later on the street. She went back to the police station that day after he walked right by her, but the staffer at the front desk told her the inspector wasn't there and wouldn't be back that day. Not long after that they called her mother from Split and told her to watch out for herself and her daughter; she shouldn't be putting them at risk. Every few years, with the changes in government, she'd try again, but every time, no matter how she went about it, she'd be faced with the same wall. She was reluctant to burden Nora. Though she could see that Nora saw and understood everything, they never spoke of it. Then she got her first dog and wandered off on longer and longer walks by the sea. They each managed by living in what each could handle; too great an intimacy would have undercut the monotony of their everyday lives, and losing the monotony would have made things unbearable. By the time Nora was fully independent, the distance between her and her mother had grown, and there was no longer a way back. The door had already long since been shut. All that was left was to feign an average existence, to turn herself into the Nora who studies, the Nora who works, the Nora who goes out with friends and gets into superficial relationships that never go on dangerously long. She succeeded in repressing all the names linked to what happened to her father, though they did occasionally resurface, when a political party needed to trot out the never-resolved incident. She shielded herself from thoughts about it, while doing everything—as if following the ABCs of textbook psychology—to bring herself back to it. She studied journalism, planned to work on research, took a job at a political weekly.

While she was doing what she could to access the Internet and read the emails from her editor, she noticed Josip Ilinčić sitting at one of the nearby tables, and it flashed through her mind that perhaps this was the very table where Oliver had sat. Over the last two decades everybody had come to think of Ilinčić as the local sheriff; evidence had never been put forth that he'd committed any crimes. He dabbled in all things war-related and the war's aftermath. In the postwar years, the focus was on privatizing what had been public property. Through one of his more controversial moves he became proprietor of the Hotel Danube. He glanced over at her; nothing about her held his attention—or maybe, if only for a moment, the sight of the laptop on the table. Nora eyed his half profile: he was sitting there in a black leather jacket, a cell phone in each hand. On the table in front of him there was nothing but a glass of mineral water. She felt an inexplicable repulsion at the way he commanded the space around him. His legs were long and sprawling; the low armchair he was sitting in was too cramped for him. As if he felt her eyes on him, he looked up from his two cell phones and eyed her over his eyeglasses. Nora didn't flinch; she gave the slightest nod. Then she went back to the screen, which kept refusing the password. She looked around for the waiter. When he saw Nora gesturing, he rose sluggishly from the bar stool and ambled over at a lazy pace.

"Sorry; the password doesn't seem to work for the Internet."

He didn't say a word, just sighed deeply.

"I tried several times," continued Nora, "but it won't take."

"I'll bring you another one," he said reluctantly.

While the waiter was on his way back to the bar, Ilinčić, who was now watching Nora with interest, summoned him with the snap of his fingers, whispered something to him, and sent him off. The waiter disappeared behind the bar, and when he came back to Nora's table he was noticeably more courteous.

"There; this should work,"—he put a slip of paper on the table— "and the boss wants to know what you'd like to drink."

"Oh, nothing, thanks, no need. I just wanted to check my email; I'm about to leave." She leaned forward as she spoke, with a grateful wave to the boss.

"A quick drink; come on . . . you don't want to hurt his feelings," insisted the waiter. Ilinčić was already on his way over to Nora's table with a frozen smile.

"Please—I'm grateful for the offer, but no thanks." Nora didn't understand what he hoped to accomplish by insisting.

"Aren't you our guest?" asked Ilinčić when he reached her table.

"Yes, but no need . . ."

"How long are you staying, if I may ask?" Ilinčić eyed her openly.

"Another day, maybe two," she answered briefly.

He nodded without taking his eyes off of her, then he reached into an inside pocket, took out a laminated business card, and offered it to her. She took it, read the name and title, and then looked long at his face. There was something reptilian in his gaze. Long ago she'd read a book about the work of the brain and remembered the part about the difference between the brains of mammals and reptiles. The limbic part, key for emotions, was lacking in reptiles and was to blame for what humans called a "lack of affect." The missing piece.

"And you are . . . a tourist?"

"A journalist," she answered, and then extended her hand. "Nora Kirin."

She hadn't expected the transformation. Ilinčić pressed her hand, and there was still no sign of anything in his eyes, but his lips quivered strangely, and he tried to mask this by lickng them.

"From around here?" he blurted.

"No, from Omiš," Nora answered evenly, feigning confusion. The last thing she needed was for him to tie her to Osijek.

"I see . . ." mumbled Ilinčić.

"Here we are, a little cherry cordial for the lady." The waiter inserted himself into the narrow space between the two of them.

"Well, thank you." Nora raised the glass and tossed it back. "I'm off to the poetry reading." She slipped her laptop into her backpack and returned to her room, skipping steps. She couldn't explain what had brought on such a feeling of discomfort that she'd fled without even checking her email. As soon as she shut the door behind her and was in her room, she turned on the shower and ran it for a long time; the water was only tepid, and under the light it looked yellower and yellower. The water pressure was so weak that after she'd showered she felt no better. Still, she decided to dress up a little for the poetry reading. She combed her hair, put on mascara and lipstick, replaced her loose black top with a tighter-fitting one. She felt anxious about parting with her laptop. Everything she had was on it. But she slipped it under the blanket—as if that would be of any help. She put on her coat in the hallway, and on her way out she peeked once more into the restaurant. Ilinčić was still sitting there with one cell phone to his ear and the other in his hand.

6.

She and he and he and I

we're at the border
and there's no way back

before (spring 2010)

When it was dark in the stairwell, he lingered by the front door of her apartment, listening for the sounds coming from within. His heart pounded in the dark, and he heard his temples drumming. No one passed that way for ten, fifteen minutes at a time, and in his thoughts he ran through the scenes from several days before on the other side of Kristina's door, on the kitchen floor and in the hallway. He was focused on the one point in time and space from which his entire life, the reason for his existence, had crystalized. He framed each individual scene, broke them down into second-long segments, and then stretched each one to infinity. The whiteness of her skin, the lock of hair he brushed from her brow, her eyes moving under her lids as he entered her, over and over. That point became his center. Now he needed to push aside everything that was blocking his way to Kristina and the future that lay before them. He'd only seen her once since then, while she was getting out of her car out in front of the building, her hands full of shopping bags, fumbling with the belt of her coat. Their eyes met, and just at that moment Ante got out on the other side of the car. They didn't greet each other, but he knew that this was because she wasn't alone; he hadn't lost hope. Yet. She was still on sick leave; he was worried that she'd never come back to teach him: the school year was almost over. At school he was at least able to see her every day, openly, soak in her every word and gesture, and nobody would think it strange. After all, that was why he was there in class, to see her and hear her. Now he was working to get to know the regular rhythm of Ante's departures and arrivals. The sequence changed from day to day, but Ante never spent much time at the apartment. Most evenings he was out; he'd come back at different times, sometimes at midnight and sometimes at five in the morning. Dejan longed to visit her again, but he worried about endangering her; he assumed she was already in deep over her head with problems, especially thanks to his mother. The infamous Thompson concert was on that very evening, commemorating the founding of the First Brigade, which had started all of this. But, again, if it hadn't been for him mustering the courage to visit her in her apartment, knowing she'd be alone, maybe none of this would have happened, maybe he never would have dared. Three floors above her he smoked by his window, and from his bedroom he watched the parking lot, expecting to see them come out of the door together at some point, get into their car, and leave for the concert. After a time, instead, he noticed a figure limping toward the car: Ante. He was alone; he got in and, without waiting for anybody, he drove off toward town. Dejan assumed he wouldn't be back soon. He didn't stop to think; he flew out into the hallway, grabbed his jacket for appearances' sake. From the dining room, he heard:

"Where are you off to now?"

"Out," he barked.

"Where are you going, Dejan?"

"Off for a walk, okay? Want to come along and hold my hand?" he snapped at his mother, although this wasn't like him.

"Fine, son, no need to shout; do as you like! Just relax."

Dejan was already out the door, skipped down to the ground floor, went out through the main entrance, and looked up. Olivera was in his room, in the same pose at the window where he'd been just minutes before. He knew. He circled around the building and came back in the door on the other side, climbing up the fire escape to the second floor. He didn't turn on the light, but didn't stand long in the dark this time. He knocked softly on the door, hoping she'd hear, maybe more feel than hear, and open the door before someone came along. He couldn't hear anything from inside, but just as he raised his hand to knock once more, the door opened. He was allowed to enter without resistance. The apartment was a mess. Chairs were tipped over; he could feel shards of glass under his tennis shoes, the reek of alcohol from the rug and sofa. Kristina was sitting, curled up on an armchair, hugging her knees, her chin tucked behind them. The only light in the living room shone from the muted television, so her figure in the corner seemed tiny and childlike, her hair loose; of her face all he could see were her eyes peeking out over her knees. Shocked by the sight, Dejan sank slowly onto the sofa, fingering the wet stains, and didn't dare come closer.

"What happened here?" he asked softly, after he'd mustered the courage to take her in with a look.

"I didn't want to go to the concert," she said calmly.

"So he trashed the apartment."

"He'd have trashed it anyway," she said with a bitter smile.

"Did he touch you—"

"No," she said.

"You can't go on like this."

"Why did you come?" she asked him coldly. She stared past him, and he couldn't take his eyes off her. She loathed herself for everything, especially for agreeing, at the meeting with Ilinčić, to him representing her if the investigation resulted in her suspension. She went along with the story that she was the victim of a resurgence of Serbian hostilities, even though she knew for a fact that this was the work of one crazy woman and several brainless, impressionable parents. Deep down she knew Ilinčić and his crowd were the ones who needed this story the most, and she could clearly see how such stories begin. On the other hand, Ante was drinking more and growing increasingly aggressive, and she hadn't lifted a finger to help him. And moreover, she had a powerful desire to push him even deeper down than he'd ever been, to a place he'd never come back from. Most of all she hated herself because Dejan's company felt so good, although she'd reached the point of nausea at least twice daily since that day.

"Kristina, I love you," he said, his voice shaking.

"Come on—you 'love' me," she shot back sarcastically. "You have no idea what you're saying." All her bitterness came pouring out against him, mostly because it could, but this didn't sway him in the slightest.

"We have to get away from here together." He could think of nothing else.

"But where? How? What would we do? Have you thought about that? Do you imagine he wouldn't find me? Come on— this would be too much for him; he'd kill me for disgracing him like that. I can only hope the drinking kills him, somehow."

Dejan hadn't given much thought to all this; he felt something would turn up for resolving things, but only if they were together, and her mistrust hurt him. All his strength deserted him when she was so cold. He moved up to the edge of the sofa where he could reach her and took her hand. He was afraid she might push him away, but she made no effort to resist. He kissed her hands, then moved over to the armchair and, hugging her, he took her in his lap. Then everything was good; the sum of all forms of love and hate in their exchange was equal; they canceled each other out, and in the process they were able to approach—perhaps not together, but each separately—a place that drew them away from where they had just been.

"I'll come up with something," he promised, whispering in her ear, while they lay on the alcohol-soaked sofa. He nuzzled up to her, while she stared at the ceiling, turning her face away from the fragrance of his hair.

"I won't leave you alone, not ever." Damp and sweaty, he pressed up against her.

"Go now," she said, leaving no room for doubt, looking him straight in the eye.

"Fine, I'll go; don't worry." He was trying to give her everything he had.

"Oh, come on; this will sort itself out somehow." This was the most tenderness she could allow herself and the most she had for him. She saw him to the front hall, suffering the little shards of glass in her bare feet without a sound. She didn't want him there anymore, just as strongly as she wished herself somewhere else. She could even disappear, whatever. When she shut the door behind him, her eyes went to the safe in the hallway.

7.

Money in hands

buy me sell me
money in hands

then, recent (fall 2010)

On the cell phone screen there were twenty-seven missed calls. There had been at least as many every day, sometimes more but never fewer, ever since the daily papers published the transcript of the conversation, and then the most riveting parts of the recording were played on the evening news. Brigita had expected the mayor's reaction and that it would be violent, but the leader of her political party promised she'd be protected in every possible way and she could count on a term of office at city hall, later maybe even in the Assembly, and he tripled all the mayor's other offers. All she had to do was keep her head down for a time until the worst of the storm blew over. But the mayor did not give up, no surprise; first he denied everything, then he declared the recording doctored, then he claimed amnesia, and finally he began calling her day and night. It made no difference when she changed her number; within twenty-four hours he'd unearthed the new one. At one point she'd had enough; she didn't feel so much intimidated as irritated and hopping with adrenaline. When the phone rang for the twenty-eighth time that day, she picked up.

"Hello?" she said sharply. All she heard over the phone was silence, likely the mayor's confusion; no doubt he'd been dialing the number automatically and wasn't expecting a response. Then he pulled himself together.

"Ah, Brigita, darling little Brigita, where have you been? No word from you for days? Didn't we say we'd get together for coffee?"

"What do you want?"

"Listen, you were right with what you said about the friendships between men and women; it looks as if this old mule was all wrong . . ."

"Please stop calling. Things are as they are. You didn't leave me much choice."

"Really? Not the way I saw it, Brigita darling . . . But know what? I'll give you what you so nicely call a 'choice.'" He laughed bitterly.

"Meaning?" She wasn't about to beat around the bush.

"I'll leave you the choice of rescinding this in public, admitting you set me up, or of having your kids read in the papers the truth about their mother."

"No point in threatening me; you'll get nowhere with that," she snarled.

"Oh, I'm not threatening; heavens no, Brigita. Just want to be absolutely sure you're good with a charming little piece coming out in the next day or two about the beginnings of your career at the InterContinental massage salon? So adorable, I must say!" Brigita was about to respond, but she froze. Quickly collecting her thoughts, she waited to hear what else he had up his sleeve.

"I've got the pictures, see?" he sneered. "What about that coffee, now? Eh?"

"What pictures?" she asked coldly, and he could tell she was suddenly concerned.

"From your youthful years, darling little Brigita! Sweet as candy . . . cutting quite the figure with that baseball bat . . . If only I'd known this earlier, I'd have been so much smarter. But who'd have guessed! And a teacher, no less!"

"What do you want?"

"All I'm asking is for us to get together for coffee, Brigita darling. It's worth our while, for both of us. The damage may still be fixable. What do you say? Maybe you were just having a little fun? You do so love a laugh . . ."

"When?"

"Tomorrow night at ten, out by the hangar."

"Fine," she answered dryly and hung up.

She should never have picked up. He was probably bluffing. There couldn't be any pictures; nobody knew anything about it. Except for the Boss, who was dead, and Schweppes, who'd taken the pictures, and her. It was only for a brief time. She hadn't had the sleaze to see it through, though the offers poured in from everywhere. One drunken night at the casino, after her shift, the Boss sidled over to her table. His eyes swam with an oily gaze, and at his side swung the rounded end of his stained wooden bat. In his other hand he held a leather leash, leading a German shepherd with a muzzle over its shiny black snout. The dog watched her, its head cocked to the side. The boss stood in front of her and dropped a big roll of bills onto the green felt tabletop. She wasn't sure what he had in mind. He came up to her and, with his clammy breath, said:

"To make an ad for the business." Then he winked, took her under the arm, and led her down to the basement of the casino where the massage salon was.

A stage set had been arranged. A red cloth backdrop hung on a frame and stretched across the floor for six, seven feet. Two small reflectors had been set up on the sides. On a nearby table there were collar-shaped bracelets, a bow tie, a few items of black lingerie, and a silk blindfold. The Boss pointed the bat at the lingerie and said, tersely:

"Do it."

Brigita went behind a partition and started unbuttoning her clothes, hands trembling. She made no attempt to object, though she was seething. She chose three items and put them on: the collar-shaped bracelets, the bow tie, and the black, see-through panties. She stepped out and almost blithely asked: "What now?" looking the Boss right in the eye. He swung the wooden bat and tossed it to Brigita. She caught it deftly.

"Now have fun," he said, arching his eyebrows. Then he dropped into an armchair and let the German shepherd off the leash. Holding the greasy bat in her hands she felt strange, but not bad. She stood, covered in gooseflesh, in the middle of the cold room.

"Need inspiration?" This was the first and last time she snorted cocaine. She and Schweppes. Then he came up behind her and tied the blindfold over her eyes. She danced in the dark, sensing the pungent odor of animal fur, and he snapped the pictures. All three of them stayed in the basement room until the next afternoon. Only once did she ask Schweppes about the pictures—they were already together by then—and he swore he'd destroyed them, her face couldn't be seen on a single one; he told the Boss they hadn't turned out well. She no longer gave a thought to that night. Brigita was able to put things like this behind her. Never a thought, until today. She considered calling the party leader, then realized she couldn't. Nobody else must be involved in this. She hadn't heard in years from the only person she could have called.

℘   ℘   ℘

For nights now he hadn't been sleeping. He went out and rambled around the city, eyes glued to the pavement, while all those near to him, and at the office, went on acting as if nothing had happened. Whenever he looked up and saw, in the distance, black hair done up in a ponytail, blood flushed his face; he gasped for breath and clenched his fists. At the camp they'd called him Red. When they interrogated him before beatings, a red flush spread across his face, and their blows pummeled the patches of red. After coming back from the camp, he spent the next few years at a hotel on the Adriatic Coast. In his early forties he was granted a disability pension and declared unfit to work. Once he stood so close to the edge of the Krk Bridge, while cars whizzed by, that he felt the ease of the space between the concrete and the sea. He found staying on the solid bridge unbearably difficult, and was never able to explain the moment, except as his discovery of God. The vast amount of irrational evil he'd witnessed in his life required at least an equal measure of irrational good for a person to find a sense of balance. When he succeeded in this, he pulled himself together and, after a few years, became again what he had been, neither evil or good, neither a believer or a non-believer, a small, pragmatic man who, the more he was given the more he needed. And so it was that he began to see himself as a local powermonger who wasn't entirely bereft of ideals, but, on the way to the top, ideals regularly find their place in the theoretical realm. In practice, votes are bought, hiring is rigged, secret accounts are opened, the official's public profile is tweaked, the government is cheated at every turn. The mayor stumbled when he placed too much trust in his own preeminence and importance, just as he had trusted—in that space on the bridge between the pavement and the sea— that there really was something else beyond the sound of the buffeting gale winds. Now there was very little for him to lose. His wife had left him some time ago, she'd been living in their summer cottage over the last months. Their daughter was living abroad, and throughout the madhouse she'd only called her mother once to ask how they were doing. He was politically done for, although he found this difficult to acknowledge. When he pleaded with a colleague whose close family friend was the minister of the interior to find him *something*, he was told there was a photograph of a scantily clad woman, crouching, blindfolded, holding a wooden bat, while a large animal rocked her balance. Brigita was not easily recognizable in the picture, but if one studied it closely for a long time—and considering her biography, or so his colleague claimed—this had to be her. Younger, nimbler, and far more wanton, but her. Getting his hands on the photograph from the secret file wouldn't be easy; he didn't have the money nor was he owed a big enough favor, but even knowing that such a photograph existed was of inestimable value. The mayor hadn't made plans for exactly what he hoped to extract from her. Eating crow in public, a retraction, an admission of incompetence, anything that might reinstate him to at least some share of the power he'd enjoyed, although he'd relinquish it all just for the opportunity to throttle her with his bare hands. She had disgraced him, humiliated him, and this is what stirs the basest feelings in a person. Murders are motivated most often by feelings of shame and humiliation provoked in the murderer by the victim; all other motives rank far below these. He changed the shirt he'd worn for the last two days and nights and, checking his watch, he realized he didn't have to be anywhere in particular until the next evening. And nobody cared. He paced around the apartment, remembering the apes in cages at the zoo that were always laughing; he couldn't bear looking at them for too long. They knew full well that there was no way out for them, and there was something maniacal about their every movement, even when they were playing their usual games to see which were the stronger and which were the weaker apes.

8.

Into darkness we run

the stars hid from us
winter picked apart our bones
the wind howled loud

now (fall 2010)

Early autumns by the seaside were something entirely different; you could see the air was warmer; even the Zagreb fall was milder, monotonously subdued between the slightly chillier mornings and evenings. Although the evening wasn't yet fully dark when she left the hotel for the second time at dusk, Nora pulled the collar of her coat up to shield herself at least a little from the icy wind blowing off the river. The wind here was different from the wind along the coast, the bura, that used to chill her to the bone. Here, it chilled her head, numbed her skin, fingers, and cheeks, drew tears from her eyes. She set out for the Hotel Lav; the poet had written down the address of the place where the reading would be held. The words *Gundulićeva 19, Reading Room* were scribbled on the back of the business card. While at the hotel she'd checked on the Internet to see how to get there; Google Maps said it would be a ten-minute walk, the same as for any destination within the city. But there wasn't anything at the address resembling a reading room; the building had a deceptively mundane appearance. It was set apart by the huge flag hanging down its facade. Inside it were the consular offices of the Republic of Serbia, as well as a consular reading room where Serbian cultural events, performances of folklore, and commemorations were held. The building had belonged until recently to the son of city councillor Velimirović, who sold it to the Republic of Serbia and was given in return a three-bedroom apartment in the center of Belgrade, thereby permanently resolving several of his problems. Before this the consulate had been housed in a far more pretentious-looking building, its greatest failing being that it was built without proper building permits during the period of Serbian occupation; earlier buildings on that site had been leveled, along with their tenants. A group of a dozen or so people was gathering in the courtyard of the white three-story building, clustering in little groups; they all knew each other. Nora had the impression that most of the guests were eyeing each unfamiliar newcomer with suspicion, and were communicating among themselves with gestures and glances that were meaningful, precise. She tried to gauge the profile of the average poetry lover who'd come for a dose of aesthetic exorcism, or perhaps some of them regularly frequented the consular reading room. Through her mind flashed the thought that they all had something gray in their auras, and just then the poet spotted her, having leaped, literally, out from the shrubs next to the building. "I cannot believe it!" he exclaimed, elated. She wasn't quick enough to stop him from pressing her hand, again, to his lips. "Though I am a believer, and you must know I was hoping! Still, we'd met only once," he halted. "I won't disappoint you this evening." He did not drop her hand.

Nora simpered politely, feeling relief—after the poet's gushing performance and his mistaken impression that the two of them enjoyed a special relationship—that the people standing around them had returned to their regular consular conversations. The poet ushered her into a broad hallway and tried to wrest her coat from her, but Nora wrangled with him for several minutes and held on to her coat and purse. Meanwhile the reading room filled; when she peeked around the door she saw that all the seats had been taken. The poet was already sitting at the table facing the audience, and when he saw her at the door he gestured frantically for her to sit in the first row in one of the two remaining empty seats, right next to Velimirović. The journalist, Nikola, Velimirović's young protege, was sitting on his other side, whispering intimately in Velimirović's ear, clearly mixing business and pleasure. At first Nora shook her head politely, and then pretended she didn't understand. The poet's gestures and the gray-haired heads all turning to stare at her made her skin crawl. In the seats on either side of the poet sat an elderly woman with spiderweb-like hair and olive-hued skin, another shade of gray, with bulky jewelry strung around her wrinkly neck, and a very young man with upper-lip fuzz that was not quite ready for a shave. The young man was introduced as a member of the Sveti Stefan drama group; he would be reciting the poet's verses.

"And now we'll sketch our poet's context to help you get to know him better." The elderly moderator in her creaky voice introduced her remarks on the poet's life.

"Our Grozdan was born not far from here in the month of March—a time of year that heralds springtime and life, but that very same month the Danube River flooded the city. At the time, nobody saw this as a symbol of a *coming flood*, nor would anybody have believed that twenty-six years hence, the city would become a new Atlantis. But perhaps this is the very moment where we should seek the genesis of his creative opus, the reason why Grozdan would become a poet whose verses would capture the apocalyptic accent of our world and the spirit of rebellion. Borne by the powerful force of precognition, he unmistakably forecasts the cataclysm and the integral deconstruction of the world. He draws through aesthetic exorcism the times we have fallen victim to and their image. Meanwhile he practices the meditational techniques of Vipassana, Kundalini, Nada Brahma, and Nataraj, and has shown a growing interest in the cultures of the East," enumerated the moderator, while Nora—standing the farthest from the improvised stage at an elevated vantage point within the room, the only person standing by the door—focused on the nonverbal processes going on within the reading room. The older members of the audience, in the first rows, were struggling to stay awake and swearing to themselves that as soon as they made it home tonight they wouldn't stop to brush their teeth, or what was left of them, but would hop straight into bed. Several of the middle-aged ladies soaked up every word, their eyes wide, nodding like mechanical toys. It would take them weeks to recover from the marvels of the evening. Through the sliver of a gap between the audience members and the chairs, Nora could see Velimirović's fingers on the edge of the seat of Nikola's chair, drumming to the rhythm of the creaky voice, and the poet's impassive gaze, soaking up, chameleonlike, the romanticized paeans of praise with the entire surface of his body. She noticed one of the feet of the young man who'd be reading the verses twitch uncontrollably under the embroidered tablecloth. His voice cracked as he fought to recite "Poem to My Native City" in a loud voice, almost shouting: "They extracted you from my body as if you were my gall bladder"—bellicose, tearful, overdone.

Just then, Velimirović stood up and, hunched over with his cell phone to his ear, strode by Nora without noticing her turn to follow him, shadowlike, while rummaging through her purse for cigarettes. Velimirović moved into the depths of the courtyard while she remained hidden in the shadows under an overarching balcony. A beam of light from a spotlight on the façade of the building lit his broad shoulders, framed by the darkness and black branches. He shifted from foot to foot, and the conversation so engrossed him that he briefly perched, several times, on one foot. He spoke in a soft mumble, widening the circle of his pace through the courtyard, coming at one point right to a slender birch tree not far from Nora, who was keeping her eyes trained on him. He ran his fingers over the birch bark, tenderly smoothing the loose white ribbons, as if nursing the tree back to health, like he was in his own backyard, somewhere where the very bark of the trees and their seasonal changes were familiar to him. Nora wasn't in the mood to go back in. She was sickened by this whole circus of the unnamed apocalypse which had, floodlike, inundated the city, these people out to retailor history, to translate their bystander role into one of victimhood—and, leading the charge, the narcissistic poet flogging his story to the world. This travesty inspired in her first sarcasm, then fury, and then grief. Of Velimirović she knew what everyone knew; more or less everything he'd done was public knowledge, yet somehow this wasn't enough to damage his reputation. He'd trained as a psychiatrist and earned his medical degree in Belgrade; his professional, wartime, and political career, in Croatia, reached its peak in the autumn of 1991, when he marched into the devastated city as the officer in charge of the Medical Corps for Western Srem. He and Goran Hadžić were, in fact, the first to venture into the ruins of the hospital. As a high-ranking official, Hadžić served as a minister in the Serbian Krajina government, and at the signing of the Erdut Agreement Velimirović represented a new Serbian party formed during the transitional administration by fusing together several existing parties, to distance him from his previous party, which was illegal and notorious. This was the way Velimirović came to be a political leader. He was decorated at the infamous Bosnian Serbian headquarters at Pale by Radovan Karadžić with the Order for Wartime Services in the Danube River Valley, and only a few years later, he received another medal for his contribution to the peaceful reintegration of the Danube River Valley. The current political balance of the city often depended on him. When there were not enough votes on the right or the left to establish a majority, Velimirović stepped in, massaging to the maximum the corrupt potential of the local political system.

By now he'd noticed Nora, and out of the corner of his eye he watched her for a few seconds, and then wrapped up his conversation and came over to her.

"Lovely evening?" he asked, smoothing his beard.

"Chilly," answered Nora absently; she didn't have it in her. No longer could she stomach conventional chats with people like him.

"Like to go in? Warm up? Have a drink?" Velimirović hopped about, rubbing his hands. Applause could be heard inside.

"No, thanks, on my way out. I'm done." She tried to step around him.

"You're not refusing your host's hospitality, are you?" He leered, hyenalike.

"Well, I suppose I am. Yes." Nora was already at the gate. "Nice place!" she called back as she shut it behind her. Seldom did she muster the courage for such brash repartee, and all the way to the center of the city her hands were still trembling. She didn't feel like going back to her hotel room. Too early. The adrenaline had warmed her, so she thought she'd sit on one of the heated terraces in town and have a drink—maybe a stiff drink.

℀ ℀ ℀

Blue and green
how do I protect myself
from change?
by changing

As she came up to a crosswalk in the center of town, she wondered whose idea it could it have been to install equipment for clicking away the seconds in this impoverished city with its handful of traffic lights. She watched the seconds melt away on the digital display and wondered how much this must have cost, and whether somebody laundered money on the project, and then mused whether her perspective had become so warped that she saw malfeasance whereever she looked, unable now to enjoy even the smallest facts of life, like knowing how many seconds she'd have to wait to cross the street. Just as the pedestrian light turned green, Nora glanced at the first car waiting at the crosswalk and spotted the familiar face of the cab driver. He noticed her. She waved, relieved when he raised his hand and smiled, and then he gestured to her to cross the street. Nora stepped into the crosswalk and then stopped and leaned to his car window.

"Still here?" he shouted over the rumbling motor.

"Well, yes, I am," she answered and smiled. "And so are you," she added.

"Well, yes I am"—he nodded—"going nowhere but in circles."

The display showed she had another eleven seconds before the cars would have the green light.

"Up for something . . . ?" She surprised herself, offering *something* to a cab driver she'd only met twice in her life. He raised his eyebrows, surprised, and repeated:

"Something?"

"Well, I was thinking, coffee, or a beer . . ." she said, though she looked a little tentative.

"You bet." He was quick. "Find a place to sit over there at the 032. I'll join you once I've parked"—the rest of his sentence was interrupted by the cars behind him honking, and Nora was going to have to wait for another forty-five seconds. She'd never done that before, but for some reason she felt no anxiety, nor that she was out of line. She was grateful for a familiar face this evening, for someone she didn't know from a courtroom, the media, or the war. Caffe Bar 032 was right by the crosswalk, with nylon sidewalls around the terrace and waitresses wearing tight-fitting skimpy green dresses. She sat in the half-open section as one of the waitresses materialized at her side.

"Up for today's special?" she asked in a shrill voice, with a broad grin. "*Pelin* bitters and cola, only seven kunas!" Jaw jutting, she waited for Nora's answer.

In high school Nora had once nearly been through alcohol poisoning with bitters and cola, and she'd never tasted the stuff since, but there was something about the young woman, the hostess, and her earnest manner that made her decide to go along with it and give the bitters another chance.

"Sure, I'll go with the special," she said.

"Fabulous! And now you're automatically entered into our contest!" Her euphoria seemed almost out of control, and Nora hoped the waitress wouldn't ask anything more of her. She saw the taxi driver approaching the terrace, looking for her. He was wearing the leather jacket and jeans he'd been in the day before; he looked tired, and had a slight scowl, but when their gazes met, he smiled with his eyes.

"Excellent choice of table," he said solemnly, though they were all the same, cramped and wobbly, organized so they took up as little space as possible.

"I'm choosy," said Nora, shooting him a sideways glance.

He extended his hand over the table, looking her straight in the eyes.

"I'm Marko."

"Nora," she said. "Once again, though you knew that."

"Have you managed to uncover anything for your story?" he

asked, sitting across from her; apparently, he remembered every detail from their two brief encounters.

"Not much." She stopped, and then chose to be sincere: "What is there to uncover? A tragic story people are getting off on, the mob who think they're better, smarter, more ethical, that it could never happen to them. All in all, miserable people."

"Yes, I agree." He sounded as if he could see everything clearly. "But why, then, write about it?" He really wanted to know.

"Well, I have to. I work for the press"—she smiled—"and the real stories, the ones with something real to uncover, aren't assigned to me."

"Annnd heeere cooommmes the *pelllin*!" crooned the hostess in screechy tones, and leaning over the table, she shoved her overexposed breasts in Marko's face, smiling flirtatiously. He moved back, with his chair, to make room for her.

"And for the gennntlemaaan? Will you try today's little special?" As he moved away, she moved toward him.

"No, thanks; I'll take an espresso." He did what he could to look around, not at, her, though this was nearly impossible.

"Whaaat a shaaaame; what about a selfie with the two of us?" She flung her arm around his shoulders and reached into the pocket of her apron for her cell phone.

"Oh, no, truly no need." He was polite but firm, although she was already pressing up against him. A smile escaped Nora, which he noticed, and it softened him.

"Hey," began Nora, "so, you drive a cab, and this is a place you like." She was teasing him a little and that made him smile. She realized her tone was perhaps a little too familiar, and that stopped her for a minute. "Sorry, I'm talking to you as if we're old friends; but then again, we're about the same age. Are you from around here?"

"More or less," said Marko, smiling. "A childhood in a boring city nobody ever heard of until the war, then a go at being a student, then the army, then the black-hole time, then the cab in what is once again a boring city. The story of our generation, one you probably know."

"Yes, for the most part." Although he seemed like a straight-forward, self-possessed man, Nora had the feeling there was a lot more there than just boredom and the story of their generation, but she was reluctant to press. She just wanted them to keep talking; it felt good.

"Well, fine; what do you think?" She switched the focus to what she was currently dealing with. "From the perspective of a boring cab driver, what was actually going on among the three of them?"

"Nobody except the three of them can know for sure, but as you said, the story is tragic. No point in turning this into an interethnic conflict, though unfortunately it will, clearly, be used for that by all sides." He was deeply aware of where he lived.

"Where were you during the war?" Nora couldn't stop herself from asking. She assumed he was in the army, and then maybe, like she, a refugee at a hotel on the coast.

"Here," he answered plainly, and then looked her in the eyes. At first Nora didn't get it.

"What do you mean, 'here'? During the war?"

"Yes, during the war."

"And afterward, too?" She was still groping to understand.

"Afterward, too."

"Oh, I see." Only then did she get it: Marko had been here the whole time, and yet she'd been thinking he was a Croat. She couldn't have said why; in fact, there was no reason to have taken it for granted that he wasn't a Serb. She drank down a big sip of her bitters and cola—every bit as disgusting as when she was in high school—and struggled to come up with what to say to keep the conversation going. She was afraid of what he'd say. She felt sure he'd come up with something along the lines of *Is that a problem for you?* and then things would get all awkward, but he didn't. For a time both of them were quiet.

"So, what was that like?" she asked him. For the first time she was talking with someone who'd spent his youth in the city when it was razed to the ground.

"Bad. Thugs everywhere, people shooting guns all the time. The inflation devoured everything, the bread tasted like a kitchen sponge. We could see the lights of cities in the distance—Osijek, Novi Sad—and dreamed about what it must be like where there was electrical power, while here we were being fed the line that we were finally free." He smiled gently. He was showing no restraint in responding to her questions; he wasn't evasive or pretentious, his answers—candid. Nora listened, and then asked more questions. She couldn't remember when someone's story had so engaged her, when *someone* had so engaged her, and Marko was talking as if he were saying these things for the first time. About the city he hadn't moved from, except to go around in circles. He said little about himself and mostly talked about the mood and the time, the people who'd disappeared. Nora talked about the coast, her recollections of the apartment they never came back to, her father who was killed in the war. Marko didn't ask for more than she was willing to say; he just listened, especially to what she wasn't saying. The hostess hovered near them several times, but neither of them noticed her. The terrace soon cleared out, and then they were the only guests left in the café. They didn't feel like going, but there was no particular reason to stay, except for their conversation which was unfolding outside of the time and context in which they found themselves, and there was still so much to talk about. Closing time was near; the waiter had already begun threading the cord through the table legs of the tables near them, hurrying to finish his shift.

"We really ought to be moving along . . ." she said, not entirely convinced.

"Yes, it's late; nobody works after eleven here."

"I'm guessing the party I was at before we ran into each other is still hopping, but there's no point in going back there." She smiled at the very idea.

"What party?" Marko asked.

"Oh, a reading from an awful book of poems at the Serbian consulate. A madhouse. Really," she said with a conspiratorial nod.

"How did you end up there? Poetry lover?" he teased.

"Well, more a case of phenomenological research. A real vampire's ball—with City Councillor Velimirović leading the charge." At her mention of the name, a shadow crossed Marko's face, and his mood changed to serious.

"Not the best company, Nora," he said seriously. "Watch out for guys like him."

"Why, do you know him?" His remark interested her, especially considering that Marko was a Serb.

"I know them all, far better than I'd like," was all he'd say.

"Oh, they're all the same. On both sides," added Nora.

Marko looked in silence at the table in front of him; he seemed dark again, as he'd been when he arrived. He reached for the cigarettes, quite close to her hand and the lighter she was holding, and asked, with his eyes, if he might use it. Until then he hadn't been smoking. With the edge of his palm he brushed her fingers and Nora thought how warm his skin was against the night air which was turning brisk. He exhaled smoke, looked at her, and said:

"There aren't two sides. You must know that."

She looked at him, her eyes questioning.

"Here in the city, as nowhere else in the world. There aren't two sides. You're either with them on the inside or you're out, and then you're outside of everything. Alone, mostly. The political parties here are merely an illusion which has reached the point of seeming to be real. And that's why all of this is as it is."

She understood him, though he wasn't speaking of any one public figure or party in particular; the clarity of his thinking worked its way into her mind, through her skin, under everything. She had the feeling that he was dragging behind him two tons of something dark, heavy, and fierce, out of which he spoke. She had the sense that he knew much more about the people and goings-on in the city than he let on. During the evening she noticed how his way of speaking was a combination of the words and phrases used by both sides. He sounded so natural, she thought, maybe that was why he was easier to understand than the others; his language hadn't been broken. When the entire world they'd lived in collapsed, the language they'd spoken collapsed, too, and after that, thinking was no longer as easy. With your language broken, with all the words that are now out of bounds and proscribed, how is it even possible to think? Marko took what he needed and was unfettered in doing so, speaking softer or harder as the moment suited him. All this went through her head as she listened to him talk.

"Velimirović and Ilinčić are sustaining an illusion? Is that what you want to say?' she asked, nudging him to be specific.

"Stay away from those men, Nora." His voice went deep and quiet.

"I can't," she blurted. She hadn't meant to say that. She'd told him nothing about her father except that he'd been killed, nor how Ilinčić's name had long been associated with the case of the murder of the Osijek policeman. Nor how she'd been circling around all these people, trying to persuade even herself that her trajectory was random, while at the same time inching closer to them, step by step.

"They've destroyed everything," she said.

"I know. So don't let them destroy you," he warned her gently. "Shall we?" He stubbed his cigarette.

"Let's," she agreed. "Thanks for your company." She felt a need to say something like that, though nothing of what they'd exchanged this evening fit into usual conventionality.

"I'll see you to the hotel." This didn't sound conventional; it sounded natural. The waiter, already in his coat, was waiting for them to leave so he could lock up. There was nobody left in town, the rutted main street under the streetlamps looked like a fresh scar on deeply creased skin. They walked along side by side, their steps loosely coordinated, occasionally losing the rhythm when stumbing over the chunks of broken pavement. Marko walked with his hands in his pockets, but then all at once Nora slipped hers into the empty space between his body and his elbow. She was tired of losing the rhythm, and this was a simpler way to walk. Marko didn't say a word, he didn't look at her, he didn't betray that anything had changed, but she felt him press her arm to his body. They no longer noticed. The walk to the hotel took no more than five minutes in real time; the other dimension eluded calculation. They stood in front of the entrance to the hotel building, where not a single light was on.

"Will you give me your number, if I need a cab?" She glanced at him out of the corner of her eye.

"Of course," he nodded, and added: "I'm here for you any time."

She entered the number in her phone and put it back in her backpack.

"Well thanks, again." She didn't know how to say goodbye. "And for seeing me back—after all, I went with the special." She extended her hand in a parting gesture. He clasped it and held it longer, more tenderly, then released it.

"Take care, Nora." He pulled her to him, hugging her with his other arm. "And don't stay here long," he whispered to her through her hair.

She nodded in his embrace and then turned and left. She thought about how she still had so much to do in the city.

9.

A few years for us

do you know how I want to find you
do I know what I need to know
love me like you've never loved

before (early summer 2010)

One of the Croatian war veterans, Zolja, ended up in a coma that night. He hurt his head badly when he slipped and whacked his temple on the steel footrest under the bar. There was shoving, shouting, spitting, heated words, but when the men in blue charged into the café, everyone's eyes went bloodshot. They were particularly touchy about this, *our* cops facing off against *our* war veterans, and why? Those damned Cyrillic signs.

Ante and his buddies gathered that night where they usually gathered, at Ferrari, had a little to drink, and then went off to patrol the city. Out in front of a city building a young greenhorn, a local cop, legs akimbo, stood on guard under the sign in Cyrillic, his hands on his back. His balls visibly shook when he saw them stopping, but when they started throwing stones and chanting their rallying cries, the kid pulled out his nightstick and lunged at Zolja. He struck him several times on the back, and since Zolja was already a little unsteady on his feet, he buckled. The rest of them swarmed the young cop, but he'd already managed to say something into his Motorola, so soon shouts were heard from a side street; the police station was only minutes away. Ante flung Zolja's arm over his shoulder and all four of them staggered back to Ferrari. They were pumped with adrenaline, feeling like they'd felt in the old days, and Maki, the barman, showed them pictures he'd managed to snap on his cell phone, showing Zolja being beaten.

"Goddamn, this goes straight to the newspapers tomorrow morning!"

Soon they figured out who the shithead was who was wearing *our* uniform. His name was Saša; nobody cared that he was ethnically Ruthenian, they'd find him. And then, not even an hour later, *our* cops came charging in to question everybody who knew something about the attack on Croatian policeman Saša.

"Fuck your mother!" shouted Zolja, a finger-thick blood vessel popping out on his neck.

"Come now, boys!" came from the other side, from the phalanx of cops. Just when Zolja was about to heave a bottle at them, he slipped on the beer-slick floor, fell and gashed his head deeply. He stayed there, on the floor, and for the first few seconds they thought he'd dropped off to sleep, and then dark, greasy blood began spreading under the tips of their shoes. They lifted him up; he was covered in blood, and they could have pushed two fingers into the hole in his skull. Ante told all this, firsthand, to Ilinčić, who listened closely, his hands folded. His fingers tapped the tip of his nose, and his thumbs stroked his freshly shaven chin.

"We'll go out there again if needed; there're plenty of us!" Ante wrapped up the story.

"Hold your horses, Ante." Ilinčić shook his head.

"Why the hell not; should we let them pick us off one by one? What's happened to you, old man? You used to have balls!"

"Ante, don't you worry about my balls. Wise up. You can't go around the city beating up cops; you aren't barbarians!"

"The kid lunged at us, I'm telling you!"

"I believe you, I believe you . . . but you know, what if that hadn't been Saša? And what then? You'll kill all of them one after another? This stinks. And here, I'm reading in the newspaper that Zolja's blood-alcohol content was at 0.2 percent. You were obviously, all of you, drunk as dogs."

"Well, we did have a drop to drink, sure . . . We're not children!"

"This stinks. That's all I'll say about it. Your actions are doing harm, Ante. You should be more in-tel-li-gent. Are you listening?" He laid his hand on Ante's shoulder. Ante nodded.

"Here, let's take, for example"—Ilinčić moved in his seat, leaned forward, and seemed about to say something important—"your wife."

"What about my wife?" Ante started.

"Why, the business with the school, the way they're harassing her—"

"They are idiots! I know them, that crazy woman, Vujanović." Here he compressed his lips and gulped. "And my wife is an idiot; all over those kids, as if they're hers. But she can't be made to see reason."

"Hey, shut up, Ante, and listen to what I'm saying." Ilinčić interrupted him and then, for a few moments, scratched his face in silence. "We can use this."

"What?" asked Ante, confused. "My wife?"

"Yes, your wife. That's the least you can do, for all of us, see?"

"She won't go along with this. Damn it, she even defends them!"

"Come now, why wouldn't she, Ante? I've had a word with her; she will, of course she will. Be smart about this. Let her go to the media. Let everyone see how things stand for us here: Our teachers. How we're being told not to attend concerts of our own songs. How we have to be careful not to go overboard in showing how much we love our country. That's our path, Ante. Not stone-throwing and boozing, you know; use that noggin of yours . . ."

"But what now; what can I do to her? I don't like the idea of violence."

"No violence, for God's sake, Ante. I'll take care of this; you just voice support when it's needed. Get it now?"

"Got it. And thank you. You're the real deal, our man."

"Always have been, always will be," said Ilinčić as he stood up, and then he swatted Ante across the back of his head. Ante was left sitting and thinking how to win over his wife. This soured him, again; he simply could not understand how she could be so gullible and stupid. She was stuck to proving the truth, as if there were such a thing, and as if anybody cared. And because of her pigheadedness, he had to admit he was actually a little pleased that all this was happening to her. Let her see what it was like when she didn't listen to him; maybe that would wise her up. Luckily there were still people like Ilinčić who, despite his high-level position, was willing to go the extra mile for the cause. He decided not to force anything, but he'd be a little tougher on his wife. She used to be more attentive, make the effort, try to please him. He was the one who found her the job as soon as they returned to the city. He was some ten years older and was pleased to have a younger wife. But then, bit by bit, she began talking more about a *normal* life. *When are we going to start living like normal people?* That was how she put her questions to him, but what did she mean by *normal?* Was he supposed to forget all that had happened and how it happened? If there hadn't been me, goddammit, there wouldn't be you. And so on and so forth. While the war was on, everyone treated him with awe and respect, but now, wherever he went, it was as if he were a leper. *What? You expect kid-glove treatment?* Damned right we do! Fuck your goddamned mother. *That* was normal, not this. The minister in charge of war veterans wants to assign the veterans, us, to serve as marshals for a gay parade! Hey! Who ever heard of such a thing! What have they done to earn the gratitude of this country?! Butt-fucking, most likely. Ante was still ramped up; ever since he'd stepped in Zolja's blood, all he wanted was for all those who didn't respect him and didn't understand him to get the hell out of his line of vision. He wanted to go back to the front lines, and then, when he came home, everyone would weep for joy that he was back. He wanted to be back with his boys again, boys he could look in the eyes and know he'd never have a bond like that with anybody else. We faced death together; who cares about wives, fuck them. The only place he didn't return to in his thoughts was the prison camp; he'd repressed that part: the empty circle around him and his thick, warm socks, the way some of the former prisoners looked away when they passed by him in town, his first encounter with her, when they were living in the same apartment building. He missed her, later, and wanted to kill her, later.

And now he had to put up with this shit, people laughing at him. One day he saw schoolchildren on the tanks that stood like trophies at the entrance to the city. They were climbing around on them and making faces, taking each other's pictures in silly poses, giving the finger, those little bastards; they had no idea what it had been like to stand in front of a tank. To soothe his thoughts a little he started leafing through the newspapers, and then he saw a statement from the veterans' minister regarding the incident the night before. The heading read: *It was the booze that knocked him down, not the Croatian cop!* He closed the paper, crumpled it into a ball, and went home to his wife.

⚜   ⚜   ⚜

Circle
the wind thinks
the wind knows
everything we know, you and I
it loves me
it carries me
it smashes me

What with his connections in Osijek, people in the city and in the national administration he'd found jobs for or who owed him a favor, it wasn't difficult to come up with an inspector who'd suspend the teacher and coax this thing along. To our benefit, of course. This was, after all, for her own good. She'd be fine. For a time she'd be out of work, sure; she'd be the rallying cry for our struggle. A good thing she has an education, and then he'd find her a job in a better, ethnically pure school. One day she'd be grateful. When the suspension was announced due to her alleged irregularities and her overstepping of the bounds of her job as teacher, the Serbian parents finally went wild. They demanded her ouster, filed a lawsuit against her; the path was open for them. Through all of this, Ilinčić, indirectly, was the one pulling the strings. If the inspection had come up with a different finding, everything would have quickly died down. Kristina would have been brought back to work. But as it was, the situation veered off in a different direction. The school was besieged, teeming with journalists and representatives of non-governmental organizations. Nikola Vrcić, the junior reporter, took down statements from agitated parents, and apparently the teacher had been systematically abusing the students for years, but out of fear that their children might bear the brunt in school if they complained, the parents had been afraid to speak up until now. She'd insulted them, mocked them, said that it was better for them to leave the city as soon as they could, that this would never be their home. The situation was pushed up to the highest level, and with it Kristina's despair. By then she was living in complete isolation. They'd all abandoned her, everyone but Dejan. He came by regularly, they found a rhythm; theirs were the mornings whenever he was at school on the afternoon shift. He'd enter her quickly, convulsively, miserably, and afterwards she'd sob for a long time in his arms. Each of them took from the relationship what they needed;

he was convinced he loved her and would give his life for her, her softness, her inner warmth, the place between her breasts where he laid his head. She had a person to comfort her, to sacrifice everything for her, to trace the shadows on her face— someone who wouldn't hurt her. She'd completely forgotten that he was seventeen. She refused to think about it. He told her how they'd leave there together as soon as he finished high school and go somewhere far away, the Netherlands, maybe, or Sweden. When he came of age, only a half year from then. Nobody would look at them sideways there. He was prepared for anything; he wouldn't even mind starting out with a gas station job, or, like his uncle in Stockholm, delivering furniture, driving a truck, anything, just so the two of them could be together on their own, far from all of this. Without second thoughts about leaving this shit-filled, weird city—and even his own mother—behind. The thought that he'd never see her again didn't dismay him. He could talk about this for an hour without stopping, about how, once he'd learned the language, he'd be able to advance in every way. He didn't need anybody but her. Kristina listened to him as if hypnotized; deep inside she didn't believe a word he said, but she did enjoy his soothing voice, colored by hope. Those two, three hours each day were her escape from the despair tightening around her throat all the rest of the time. Then at one moment she would snap out of it, come to her senses, kick him out, unable to bear herself or him, until the next day, when she let him in without a word. The sofa bed in the living room was made up as a bed all day long now; she had been sleeping on it for the last months. She could no longer bear to lie next to Ante; he flung himself onto their bed, usually drunk, seldom taking off his clothes.

She got up, cracked opened the door for Dejan, and without a word went back to the sofa. Dejan followed her, looking at her back, too far behind her to reach out and touch her. She lay back down right away, closing her eyes. He lay down next to her and began kissing her eyelids. She was still warm from sleep and very pale. He lifted her T-shirt, nuzzling into her stomach, and pulled it over his head. He heard nothing but the rustle of the cloth and his heart; he didn't hear the front door opening, instead he suddenly felt Kristina's convulsive jerk and a knee to the throat which knocked the air clear out of him. Only then did he hear the scream and feel a powerful blow to the back of his head, and then somebody grabbed him by the hair, almost lifting him up from the bed. He fell between the sofa and the sideboard, gasping for air.

"You deranged whore!" howled Ante, moving toward Kristina, lunging to smack her in the face. Kristina ducked, leaped over the armchair and side table and escaped into the hallway. Meanwhile Dejan pulled himself together and straightened up. He was ready for anything. Ante turned to him; his hands were huge, his face red, his mouth foaming. He grabbed Dejan by the neck and smashed his head into the wall.

"Call the police!" shouted Dejan, but a deafening roar at that moment sliced through his yell, and Ante slumped to the floor. He could see Kristina standing in the hall, pistol in hand, phantomlike, her face stripped of all expression. Ante was still for a few seconds, and then began wheezing. Kristina's face fractured and crumbled into a thousand pieces. Dejan stepped over Ante and took the pistol from her hand. He would not let her go into this abyss alone; he aimed at the body on the floor and fired twice more. After a time, Ante's face went slack, his forehead and cheeks finally realigned, and Dejan, standing over him, stared, horrified, as he saw his own chin, lips, and forehead surface in Ante's features; seeing Ante's face was like seeing himself, asleep, in a mirror.

10.

Time to cleanse

time to cleanse
time to cleanse
time to cleanse

now (fall 2010)

"Hello?"
   "I need you."
   "How long has it been?"
   "Twenty-three months."
   "I'm not up for this anymore, Brigita."
   "I'll never call you again. Name your price."
   "Somebody important?"
   "He's out to destroy me."
   "Fine; we should meet."
   "Wherever you say, I'll be there. I need you today."

Part Two

THIS IS THE COUNTRY FOR US

II.

Eyes the color of honey

your lips on me
your hands on me
I grip a knife between my teeth
shape-changing like an otter
strapping saber to thigh

now (fall 2010)

No lights were on; the windows were like black holes in the shabby hotel. He stared at them so long they seemed to be spilling and swelling, brimming over. Nora's room faced the water and a sandy midriver island that couldn't be seen in the dark. If she ever turned on the light. The volume of water— sluicing through the riverbed at a pace that only seemed to be slow—was not easy to see, but it could be sensed. Marko stood there for a time out in front of the hotel, and then, after a pause, headed for his apartment, turning to look away from the water. Back at the beginning, years ago now, when the war felt like a movie and a huge adventure, one of the early mornings when the mist over the river was milky and at its most dense, he gazed out over this stretch of water on his way home from sentry duty and stopped to wonder who'd been logging so much lumber and how was it possible that all the logs were floating down the river, en masse, like that. The scene drew him, and down he went along the quay to take a closer look. The logs were moving slowly enough for him to see that they were clothed in ripped T-shirts and pants, around some of them swirled tubelike ribbons of dangling white intestines that, floating, bumped, tangled, met and pulled apart, as if rehearsing a synchronized dance number. All these were men, big, brawny, but lifeless. Ever since then he didn't swim in the Danube anymore, even though the summer before the war he'd been one of the boys who felt compelled to swim across it at the end of the school year. He'd felt the river was a part of him; he identified with it, gulped it down, let it sweep him along, lost himself in the river's depths. While he was a boy, Uncle Jovica, whose house looked out over the same courtyard as his did, took him fishing, only him of all the kids in the neighborhood. All because Marko had the patience for it; he could sit for hours in silence and keep track of the minute shifts in the nature around him and never be bored; he found the river far more engrossing than snapping the tails off of lizards. Marko's father had died young, collapsed in the garden while picking cherries. Bees swarmed his face, covered his eyes; he lay in the grass, his mouth slightly open, his head flung back, the cloud of bees guzzling the sweet juice until the seven-year-old boy came out to summon him to dinner. The autopsy showed he'd had a heart defect, a minor thickening of the cardiac muscle that had waited until that summer afternoon to reshape their lives. Marko's mother was warned at the time that the defect was congenital and she should take the boy to see a doctor. His short life was split into pre-bees and post-bees. A brief spell of warmth and something indefinably sweet, and then his first clear memory—when they visited Belgrade, not long after his father's death. His anxious mother took him to the Military Medical Academy for an ultrasound of his heart; the place was all vast and cold, and the doctor's diagnosis confirmed the local doctor's suspicions. The big tin soldier, who looked nothing like a doctor to Marko, pinched him on the chin with ice-cold fingers while announcing that there was good news after all: the boy would live. His little organism pulled itself oddly together in a cardiac counteroffensive which he'd rely on in the years to come as a kind of life principle, but the soldier-doctor must have cast a curse on him, just like in a fairy tale, when, wagging the boy's jaw between thumb and forefinger, he declared: "You'll be back when the time comes for you to serve as a soldier. We'll meet again! Take care, my boy!" When the time did come, in 1990, for his military service, coinciding as it did with the start of the war, Marko did his damnedest to evade the army, using his heart defect as his excuse, but nothing worked that year: not the certificate issued by the university showing he was enrolled in the study of Slavic languages and literatures, nor his mother's terrified pleas to chop off just one finger, which he couldn't agree to because he loved playing the guitar. At the time he'd have rather died than agree to a life without music. He came home only twice from his year in the navy in the Montenegrin coastal town of Tivat, and his mother visited him there once. Over four months, the longest he'd ever gone without seeing her, she seemed to have aged at least fifteen years; in one of the rare photographs there was a brisk wind blowing at her back while she stood on a dock and, weighing scarcely over a hundred pounds, looked as if she were about to be whisked away by the wind. Marko had his arm around her and looked as if he were holding her down; he was young, with too serious a gaze, full of a prescient sense of dread at something coming, something imminent and horrible. He returned from the navy in the summer of 1991 and tried, again, to enroll at the university. His efforts resulted in little more than a trip to the chaos-ridden city of Belgrade for the entrance exam. Posters featuring Slobodan Milošević were already plastered everywhere. Marko had sold off his comic book collection so he could at least attend a music festival while he was there. When he came home he discovered his mother's sudden aging was because she had bone cancer. She could no longer stand at her station at the factory. She went on sick leave and never returned to work. For the next months, Marko stayed with her and never got around to enrolling. Meanwhile he was recruited for a unit that was a hybrid, a cross between the regular army and territorial defense, something that never officially existed, nor were there documents or a commander to prove it had; it functioned, indeed, as a link between the Yugoslav People's Army and the unruly Serb territorials. The unit was made up of mercenaries and young reservists who hadn't seen what was coming quickly enough, mustered by appeals that played on their sense of patriotism, the duty they'd sworn to uphold, and fueled by youth, inexperience, and a crushing sense of having no way forward. They were all promised financial reward at a time when nobody had a job, and *as soon as this is over, once we've eviscerated the Ustashas—in a week or two, max,* the finest medical care possible would be available to Marko's mother at the Belgrade Military Medical Academy.

The halfhearted gestures toward a truce and the negotiations which Marko attended as Velimirović's bodyguard, the musty cellar where he was forced to listen to the lewd jokes of the officers, generals, and politicians, and their perverse laughter, while he and Schweppes—a kid, just his age, who worked on the Croatian side for Ilinčić—patrolled, fully armed, by a door that was slightly ajar. They exchanged glances over their gun sights, wincing at some of what they heard. For the first time, here, through the smoke and wan light, the name Kirin came up. Only years later did he realize what they were talking about then, and what Velimirović was congratulating Ilinčić for. Then, without hardly anyone ever knowing, he saved Schweppes's life and the lives of several others: he overheard plans being hatched among the Serbs to ambush the delegation of Croatian negotiators and, with news of the putsch drumming in his ears, he persuaded the Croatian team to travel by a different route. Years later he received a message of thanks over the Spanish mobile-phone network, to which he never replied, and then found a package by the door to his apartment and in it, a bottle of Glenlivet. Months of hell followed; Marko began distancing himself from his fellow fighters in the unit and kept as low a profile as he could manage. His mother was finding it a struggle to get out of bed; without his help she couldn't even reach the improvised chamber-pot toilet in the corner of the cellar where they were sheltering from the constant shelling. For days and nights she lay on a narrow folding cot, waiting for Marko to come home and lift her. The most cherished item, the best thing, he ever received in return for his service in the paramilitary unit was a package of diapers from Belgrade, through someone he knew; all the local suppliers had run out. Whenever he had to leave on an assignment that would be taking him away for a whole day or night, he'd rinse his mother with water from a bottle over a washbasin in the basement to ease her bedsores. They were all maddened by the siege, the shooting, the lack of sleep, the reek of burning buildings, the feces, the blood, and the corpses. There was no longer any clear rhythm of day and night, the whole place lived at the unnatural pace of the shelling, bombing, dying, drinking. No one was able to leave or enter the city. This evil was bound to implode. Then Marko was ordered to organize excavation backhoes to prepare several mass graves in fields just outside of town and arrange for trucks to bring in the people who'd do the digging. He didn't fire a single shot the night of the massacre; the next night he broke into Velimirović's bedroom and defiantly jammed his pistol up into the roof of the man's mouth. The first night following what the Serb forces were calling *liberation*, which Marko and his mother had been hoping finally to spend in their apartment after three months of crouching in the basement, he went down to carry his sleeping mother upstairs to her bed. He slipped an arm under her tiny, frail body and felt the stiffened, chill resistance of her thighs. All he could hear after that was the buzzing of bees. In late 1991, he went through a long bout of depression, and he didn't pull out of it until 1997. After that he hadn't left the city, feeling he deserved to live there amidst it all and with what had survived inside him. He was resolved to stay there for the rest of his life, blaming himself for each and every victim. From that time on he worked only at physical jobs and drove the taxi, reading everything he could get his hands on. Recently he'd been able to obtain almost everything over the Internet. This was the only thing that did him good for a spell, helped him feel alive and gradually pulled him up out of his deep hole. As did music sometimes, mostly dark, dark jazz. Until this evening, when, while circling around town, he'd met Nora. He nearly drowned in her eyes. He knew her so well; she was everything this part of the world was that could never be explained to anybody from someplace else. The river water which compelled him though he couldn't bear to look at it, and the honey, and the bees, and the gardens, and all the blood that had soaked deep into the ground for miles around, knives gripped between teeth, sabers strapped to thighs. He knew everything, and he saw that she, too, sensed much of it, but what she sensed didn't come close to the unspeakable things he knew. He felt like standing out in front of the hotel till the end of his days, kneeling at her bedside in case she opened her eyes. He stepped into the little elevator in his building, and, deep in thoughts about the warm place under his arm where he still felt the glow of her hand, he chanced to look at the mirror in the neon light. With a surge of nausea he hastily looked away.

12.

Cold

time is no longer a problem for me
I know no better way, actually,
to spend it

now (fall 2010)

He moved noiselessly around the dark apartment. The front door wasn't locked, which implied that the man inside was desperate or no longer cared about what would happen next, all because of his frantic obsession with revenge. He froze in the corner of the bedroom and listened to the man's breathing in the dark, how he shuddered and moaned in a fitful half sleep. Only five paces to the bed. He cocked the pistol, muffled with a silencer, and inched toward the moans. He hadn't been doing this for a while; two steps from the bed he tripped over the electric cord for the bedside table lamp and nearly lost his balance. Nevertheless, he rested the pistol precisely on the man's temple and grabbed him by the throat to keep him from shouting. He waited a few seconds for the man to wake, allowing him only

to breathe. When he saw the man was aware enough to understand what was happening, he asked him softly and distinctly:

"Where are the pictures?"

The mayor spluttered, fighting for air, his arms flailing.
Schweppes relaxed his grip slightly.

"There are no . . . no pictures . . . I just heard about them."
He confirmed with desperate sincerity what Schweppes had
assumed—he'd been bluffing. Which did not mean that they
didn't exist in a secret dossier kept by the former boss of the
underworld. With a voice full of mercy he asked once more:

"Certain?"

"I swear," answered the mayor with a sob. Schweppes moved
back a few inches and tilted his head ever so slightly to the side.
Two seconds later, the hole was symmetrical and round, lacy
only on the edges and gray as mold. For the last time, his eyes
swept the room to be sure he was leaving behind no traces.
For years now he'd been caught up with other things, mostly
smuggling, and once Croatia's membership in the European
Union had become a certainty, people had become the hottest
commodity. There were wagonloads of desperate people, and
their numbers were unlikely to diminish. They swam, crawled,
sprinted through woods, grabbed barbed wire with their bare
hands, and the blood on their palms was the color of freedom.
All he had to do was wave the EU circle of yellow stars and
they were ready to give him every cent they had. And there was
always something, dollars, euros, all he did was clear the way, he
knew the Spačva route backwards and forwards after his time
spent in the field during the war, as well as several other routes,
and he was on good terms with local police chiefs. He never
exposed himself to danger; the kids he recruited were the ones

who were exposed, while he pocketed the cold cash. Belgrade to Zagreb, six hundred euros per head; double that to Italy. His business had taken off. The array of services he offered in the chain of human trafficking was far-reaching, though over the last month he'd kept a low profile after a deputy police chief was booted who'd been one of the crucial links in his chain on that route. From a business perspective, this thing with the mayor suited him to a tee, but never would he have done such a thing for anybody but Brigita. Schweppes belonged to a group of local professional hitmen, most of them schooled abroad. He began his training as a kid in Germany, after he was convicted of assault causing bodily harm. When he arrived in Croatia in the 1990s, only just then founded as a state, he offered his services to the secret service through the Boss and the casino at the InterContinental Hotel. Absolution for his earlier sins had to come from the powerful sponsors within the state system and the crime world, which was supported right at the highest echelons of government. A segment of the criminal elite was responsible for assassinations: suspicious traffic accidents, explosive devices attached to cars, sniper kills. One of his first targets was Kirin, a policeman. The bosses of the underground were in agreement all across former Yugoslavia: the murder of one's opponents and related criminal activity aimed at erasing any connection to the people in charge was standard practice. The war was a boon to them all. If someone from the Zemun clan was interested in having someone hit, he'd reach out to his colleagues in Sarajevo, Skopje, or Zagreb for help. He'd dispatch his hitman to do the job and then have the killer hidden in one of the other ex-Yugoslav countries. Later, the favor would be returned in kind. Faced with this system, the police were hard-pressed to link the murderer to the person who'd ordered the hit, and the investigation was made all the more complicated, and still is, by the poor levels of cooperation among the various Balkan police forces. So the vast majority of these hits remain unsolved. Professional killers who work for the state always exploit moments of crisis; they hide behind political intrigue and turmoil, and their connections with the powermongers mean they won't be exposed. Although most killers are psychopaths, Schweppes was not lacking in all human emotion. He'd killed his stepfather, and then spent the man's savings. The police quickly caught him, and it was in a German prison that his training in murder began. These were his glory days; he was so young that he was allowed to return to Croatia to serve out the rest of his sentence. So the path to the casino and recruitment by the secret services was not a long one. After his first murder it was as if a bottomless hole had opened up inside him, and he'd gone over the edge. He didn't have many choices. The genotype, phenotype, the easy accessibility of weapons and the lack of any ethical constraints in society formed him quickly, fiercely, with no way out. On his way he stumbled across Brigita, and that was as close as he ever came to a moment of atonement. He watched her as she moved among the tables, as she laid her little hand on men's broad shoulders. He wanted to shield her. Himself and her together. She, on the other hand, admired Schweppes and felt safe with him, but she didn't need him in that way, and she knew she felt best when she was on her own. Men were a means to an end, not the end itself. Meanwhile she'd earned her university degree and went where nobody else wanted to go, straight into the heart of darkness, because she knew, if she were among the first, that she'd be at an advantage over others and have the chance to set up her own network. The empire soon crumbled, and then began the legal proceedings against criminal organizations. Schweppes's name and hers both came up, but at that level she remained loyal. She appeared as a witness and testified that she knew nothing, she'd never noticed anything, she was doing the job while she studied so she could get more easily through her schooling. In the end she added that she'd noticed that her boyfriend did carry a pistol. She'd thought this a little strange, just that. But that was what the times were like, other people carried weapons, too. Here their paths diverged. There were no hard feelings, and she knew that because of all this she had the right to count on at least one more favor. She was right: whenever he thought about her, all those feelings came back to Schweppes. Although he was fully capable of standing by, never getting his pants cuffs wet while he watched people drown in the Danube as they tried to swim across it, he could not resist her *I need you*. This was completely irrational and so rare in his life, because he felt almost nothing for others, with the exception of the hatred he felt for his closest family and indifference for everybody else. And once, gratitude. For a young Serbian man who saved his life at the outset of the war by deliberately changing the route of their van. Schweppes understood that he had done nothing to deserve this. That his life had been saved by the action of the young Serbian reservist was something he only learned of years later, and that the man's name was Marko, and that he was still living here in the city. He found the man's contact information through the police, sent him a message and a bottle of the finest whisky. Now that was someone he'd like to meet again, to ask him why he'd done it. He cast another glance at the mayor's lifeless body. One more person's suffering over—that was the thought that passed through his mind as he slowly shut the door of the apartment, stepping out into the quiet hall.

13.
The first and the last day

is this only a lie?
is it only trickery?

now (fall 2010)

The message flashed onto Ilinčić's cell phone at 5:30 a.m., while he was lifting weights in the basement of the private hotel gym that had previously housed a disco. He always got up early and exercised. Despite his age, he kept himself in shape, a step ahead of everyone. His man on the police force let him know the mayor had been killed before the media got a hold of it. The message was delivered flatly, as if he wasn't sure whether Ilinčić himself was involved in some way. If he wasn't, the city's boss needed to hear about it before everybody else did, but if—which the man thought more likely—he was involved, then when Ilinčić took complete control he'd remember who'd proved loyal and reliable and kept him in the loop. The news was so shocking that Ilinčić stopped working out, straining to make sense of the unexpected murder while his pulse gradually returned to normal as big beads of sweat leached from his pores. He puzzled over this murder that he'd known nothing about and who could be behind it. He took a quick cold shower, instead of the longer one in lukewarm water that he preferred, while his thoughts turned to the little girls from the local orphanage who were ordered in on weekends for the amusement of the Forestry Maintenance crew. He dressed and went upstairs to the restaurant to have breakfast and an espresso. His suspicions circled around the poltical and criminal factions in the city, without dwelling on anyone in particular. After the recording of the bribe offer was made public, the mayor was dead politically, and for an act as radical as this murder there must be a powerful motive. The other thing bothering him was the worry that there was someone out there who'd had the audacity to aim so high, sidestepping him and his connections and daring to perpetrate something this outrageous in his city. The third was the serious possibility that he would be considered a suspect and talk would start circulating that he was implicated. Someone might well turn up who knew that Ilinčić had been pressuring the mayor to change the future lessee of the port. Very little happened in the city without Ilinčić's blessing. He had a finger in every pie. He'd placed almost everyone who was serving on the city council. They didn't dare think with their own heads, except those who were genuinely stupid, and they were easy to manipulate. Like the fanatic young hawk from the radical right-wing party who sabotaged the passing of a law regulating the holding of pigs and sheep only because the document submitted by the minority party was written in both alphabets. The kid was caught hook, line, and sinker by the nationalist program, thereby vulnerable to endless forms of manipulation. Precisely because of him and those like him, all the processes in the city had ground to a halt, and the money kept pouring in. Like when, five years ago, the national government and various funds invested millions of euros in the city's commercial zone. They built up the infrastructure to support several industrial plants, but to this day not a single one of the factories had opened. Six of the investors pulled out. Parallel to building the infrastructure, Ilinčić had built a magnificent summer home for himself on the island of Pag, and the city of Pag then became their sister city. Now focus had shifted to the port: the only company anywhere in the area that was making a profit, the only undertaking with no losses and which was not laying off its employees. Approval had finally come down from above for its sale, or, as formulated in the spirit of democracy, its lease. Whoever was running city hall when the lease of the port went through, with its annual trans-shipment capacity of over a million tons of freight, would bring in enough revenue that they would never again have to worry about their own subsistence, if, indeed, the right lessee were found. Everything had to be set up with care, the tender prepared meticulously. The chaos reigning in the city was convenient in this regard, but what with a murder investigation possibly forthcoming, the dead mayor could get in the way, too. In this sense, dead Ante could prove useful. If only the Serbian kid had been a year or so older. After the *tragedy*, Ilinčić had come up with a plan: when this administration fell, he'd install someone, again, with a strong camera presence. He'd hold the tender and transactions for the port, standing, as always, in the shadows and skimming off the cream. Now, because of the murder, things would get tricky—too many police would be poking around, and they wouldn't be the usual local cops; instead a team he didn't control would be investigating the city power structures, and he'd have to keep a low profile for a time. Journalists, scandals he hadn't staged himself, morons who'd blurt out something. He could see this coming. He didn't like it. And he didn't like the way that young woman was hanging around his hotel. He'd immediately sniffed out that she was Kirin's daughter, a female version of her father. She'd struck him as familiar as soon as he laid eyes on her, focused as she'd been on her laptop. And when she gave her name as Kirin, looking him boldly in the eyes, he'd frozen. He couldn't be wrong, even though she'd said she was from Omiš. Bullshit, from Omiš. The widow had given up, finally, on pursuing an investigation, though she'd been unexpectedly persistent, but he'd always assumed that at least the daughter wouldn't stick her nose into it. He'd already have been planning how to handle a son, but as she was the man's daughter he hadn't given a thought to her all these years. And a journalist to boot. He was not one to give credence to conspiracy theories, nor did he allow himself to be swept up into a panic, but something worried him here, too much for him to let it go—her face kept swimming back into his thoughts. What had brought her here, and why? The Kirin murder was ancient history. When the case was dredged up every few years, with each change of government, he was never too worried; he could rely on the powerful backing of the head of state. And besides, they couldn't touch him even if they chose to try, because all of the ruling elite of Zagreb, including the Supreme Court, would end up in the gutter if they did. But someone's child—now that's a different matter. This he knew at a gut level. He'd send her a message, there was no other way; he had to take steps to insure his safety. He needed to really shake her up and send her back to her Omiš with her tail between her legs. What a fucking family; some people just don't know when to stop, like that father of hers. Ilinčić had offered him everything. But no, that man was so righteous. Kirin could have moved his whole family to Germany; Ilinčić had offered him that, too. If only he'd gone off and left them to wage their wars in peace, the car accident would never have happened. And now this woman shows up. She gave him the chills; he had to shake her off as soon as possible so he could get back to work.

৯   ৯   ৯

The room was bathed in sunlight. Partly because the blinds were broken, partly because she'd slept well and woken later than she usually did, especially when sleeping in a hotel. As soon as she opened her eyes, the feelings from the night before flooded back. She lay in bed a little longer, and when she realized she was thinking in unexpected detail about Marko's hands, his nose, and how his jacket smelled, she leaped out of bed and quickly pulled on her clothes, brushing her teeth along the way. She broke into a light sweat at the thought of how much time she'd wasted. She still didn't even have a full page of copy; she'd been unable to come up with anything up to the point, anything useful. Brigita Arsovska had put off their meeting, and Nora had wasted time at the ludicrous poetry reading and later with Marko. No, that wasn't wasted time. Her third and last day, she had to wrap this up; there was no chance they'd fork over for another night at her hotel—and this reminded her she ought to call her editor, whose call she'd ignored the day before. It was still early, not yet seven thirty, so she decided to go to breakfast and then at least get her notes in order before she met with the former school principal. She hurried down the stairs and through the dark hallway and came out into the morning light of the nearly empty restaurant.

There he sat, at the same table where he'd been sitting the night before, only now he was freshly shaven and wearing a white shirt. He was leafing through the newspaper, and his cell phones lay on the table, side by side. She could smell the powerful fragrance of his aftershave, which reminded her of teenage boys. She was beginning to feel she was running into such types wherever she turned. The sense of accomplishment and a well-done job among her colleagues was often mere decoration to pretty up archetypal male rivalry. They used Macs and iPhones, but otherwise the mechanisms were unchanged. The worst part of the male principle, the jousting and the pissing contests. Whoever lost had to go to war. She'd been stopped in her tracks the other day by a story on the evening news: veterans who had clashed with police were standing, hemmed in by a cordon, and one of them yelled at the police that they'd be *seeing each other soon*, and that *the war is not over; it's only beginning!* Nobody in the crowd had a retort for this, although some of the veterans were clutching tanks of bottled gas. Observed through the prism of the society where she'd grown up and in which she now lived, the war was actually a shiny, radiant point people kept returning to; they hadn't moved on from what they still saw as a time of pride and glory. The aggression, destruction, and devastation continued, only now it was no longer about defending the country. Two decades since the war, damaging behavior was still being honored, exalted, treated as if it were holy, bringing with it a death worth hurtling toward before others beat you to it. The worst part of the male principle directly provoked the worst in the female. The action and reaction brought about woman's inexhaustible thirst for self-sacrifice and service to a destructive patriarchal system. The elderly woman, only half-alive, whom they decorated on patriotic occasions, trotting her out whenever needed, had *given* four sons for the homeland and was on display as the model mother, though she was never asked whether anybody actually *gave* their children to the homeland or whether the homeland simply came for them one day and never brought them back. A stubby, crackpot Italian watched from his small Italian town the exhilarating outbreak of war from across the shallows of the Adriatic Sea, and decided, at the age of twenty, to play at being a combatant. Three months later, he ended up at the bottom of a pit with a bullet in his brain and was given a gravel-paved street as an expression of Croatian gratitude: the Italian with a Croatian heart, the hero, the silly boy with an excess of testosterone. Nora was allergic to the phrase "gave their lives." Nobody would give their life if they were asked to in so many words, and certainly not the life of their child. The life was taken; someone committed murder, and that was all there was to it. Ever since she'd been aware of the world around her as a child she'd seen this going on, and though it tried to shape her, as it shaped so many of her dear childhood friends—she could barely remember the flavor of life from before the war—somehow she managed to hang on to a sideways perspective. She glanced sideways at Ilinčić, slowing down as she passed by him. He was just as reptilian as he'd been the day before, but this time more morose. She nodded to him in greeting, but he didn't even blink, staring straight through her. This confused her; she went over to the other side of the restaurant and sat at a table with her back to him, feeling a chill creep up her spine. Then her cell phone rang.

"Are you eating?" asked her mother.

"You won't believe it, but here I am having breakfast," answered Nora gently.

"You're right, I don't believe you, but so be it. Where have you been? You haven't called."

"I'm working on an article, so I've been all over the place; I thought I'd give you a call when I got back to Zagreb." Nora made her excuses. That was mostly how they talked, she and her mother. Not too close but never too far, either. Her mother didn't want to smother her with concern and burden her daughter with her own troubles, so she kept her distance, and Nora didn't want to burden her mother, so she told her hardly anything about herself, her real self. At one level their relationship had frozen long before everything happened, which explained the questions about food, warm clothes, weather. Although both of them, through the codes, felt every shade of mood and concern in their relations.

"But where are you, exactly?" asked her mother.

"In Rijeka, something about the shipyards." Nora sounded relaxed, although she was only a dozen miles from the epicenter of the central trauma of their lives. "How's Bleki doing?" she added quickly, with interest.

"Oh, like the old dog he is; we just got back from a walk."

"Just be careful. I'll call you in a few days; maybe I'll swing by once this crazy business wraps up."

"Oh, do; last time he barked at you as if you were a stranger, it had been so long."

"I will, Mother, don't you worry."

"Take care, Nora." Nora could tell she was about to say something more, but the silence at the other end of the line was replaced by the monotonous, intermittent dial tone. Nora, too, had been about to say something more, but she gave up. She watched her cell phone screen, refreshing it when it went to sleep. Her mother wasn't one to be harnessed by the system; she fought on alone, the way she felt was right. Every once in a while, people would show up who would encourage her to capitalize on her sterling integrity, but she refused every privilege and asked for only one thing—the truth about her husband and punishment for the perpetrator, especially for whoever gave the order. Nothing more and nothing less, even if it meant turning the world upside down. Lost in thought about her mother, she was distracted by audible whispers among the waiter, the receptionist and, she assumed, the cook. They were gesticulating and shaking their heads, and when they noticed Nora watching them with curiosity they withdrew to the side, conferring with a conspiratorial air. Nora gestured to the waiter to ask for another cup of coffee, but he didn't notice. He only came over to her table after several attempts.

"Yes?" he said, in a contrite half whisper, clearly wanting to say more.

"Another coffee, please." The waiter nodded, with such a deeply worried expression that Nora simply had to ask:

"Is something wrong?"

He lowered his gaze even more somberly, as if grateful for the question.

"What?" she added when she saw the game he was playing.

"The mayor," he said, his voice trembling, and then he stopped and stepped closer: "Our mayor was murdered."

"What?" Nora rose automatically from her seat. The waiter gestured helplessly with his arms spread wide and shook his head, staring skyward through the ceiling.

"How? When? Does anyone know who?"

"Last night, apparently . . ." As to the rest of the questions, he merely shrugged. Nora groped for the cell phone in her purse and, dialing her editor's number, she peered over the waiter's shoulder. Ilinčić had left, but she knew she would have to stay on in the city.

14.
Garden

teach me how to garden
I need my own garden

now (fall 2010)

It was as if she had all she'd ever wanted. The most compelling illusion that could possibly exist, and it came in the form of white cast-iron garden furniture strewn carelessly about the large, neatly mown lawn around the house. A house in the nicest part of town, not far from the water tower, with a charming view of the river. A branch of the powerful Danube almost in the backyard. A maid. A well-behaved twelve-year-old child who had, fortunately, inherited from her only the shape of her eyes, and a husband she could wrap around her little finger. She could never completely understand his unquestioning devotion and the simplicity with which he perceived the world and life. Barbecue on the Štrand beach, hours in the garage with old motors, and his transistor radio, twice a month in the dark, without fail. This suited her perfectly, and he was of real value to her. Despite this, she'd always predicted this would not suffice, that one day, no matter how things went, she'd find herself on this overpriced, uncomfortable garden furniture, awaiting news from the past that would plunge the entire carefully fashioned illusion about her life into chaos. She seldom allowed herself moments of introspection, but this autumn morning, after she'd given the order to have somebody murdered, she dared call things by their true name. She hadn't lied to herself with the story that she'd change, nor did she genuinely want to change, although at times she'd stare out the kitchen window with a muted melancholy when her life began to feel ordinary, proper—like when her son was born, or when she picked sour cherries along the edge of her yard to make cherry cordial, or when her husband told her about his problems at work. She felt pricks of grief up and down her spine when she wished the illusion were real, and she felt them again—as she tried to hold on to her life's harmonious, middle-class façade—when it all bored her. She'd think back on herself as she was before, on her younger years: the zing of a vodka and juice, the fragrance of mornings as they dawned—and now she merely woke up each morning and juggled, split between her external and internal life. She was capable of handling everything, though most of the time she teetered on the edge and could tell that it was only a matter of time before she'd go over it. A part of her knew there was no turning back now that her pure drive for survival was the strongest part of herself. Edgily, she kept refreshing her cell phone screen; the morning was early yet and she was sitting in the garden, drinking coffee, waiting for someone to alert her to what had happened and summon her to an emergency meeting of the city council. She'd almost forgotten about the meeting with the journalist from Zagreb who was writing about the incident with that teacher, Kristina; she couldn't remember why she'd even agreed to the meeting. This was the last thing she needed now. Within an hour, two at most, all hell was going to break loose. She needed to shake off the journalist. She tried to foresee all possible ways this could play out. She had never doubted Schweppes: if anyone could do it with the truth never coming out, he could. Now she needed to work on the crossword puzzle of the city. The president of the municipal branch of her political party and future candidate for mayor had been positioned for this only recently. He was an inarticulate young technology teacher who'd be easy to manipulate, with modest intellectual potential but highly developed brownnosing skills. The real challenges were the more seasoned figures: freewheeling, self-centered Ilinčić on the one hand and murky Velimirović on the other. With them, her imperative was to create a sturdy but invisible coalition so she could realize part of her plans. One such part was a seat at the head of the port's supervisory board—not some ordinary membership from which she'd barely get enough to cover her son's after-school activities—and along with this a directorial position which would allow her to set up her own office and, through it, a tight-knit, trustworthy network. That would do for starters. While she worked on her plans, she thought she could hear sounds coming from the house. When she turned, as much as her curled-up position allowed, she needed a few seconds to connect what she was looking at to her thoughts: a child's bare feet, unexpectedly white on the gray concrete. She found herself hypnotized momentarily by the purity of skin, which was out of place in this yard and in the world, one of the feet rubbing the other, hopping, until the boy said something. She didn't understand a word.

"Darko, what are you doing here? Why are you barefoot?"

"Mama, mama . . . Pasha—look at him." She could hardly tear her eyes from her son's feet, and when she finally did look up at his hands, she saw a large mound of limp, gray fur and jutting, stiff paws splaying awkwardly around the boy's nose. The red muzzle was covered in parts by a thick, partially caked foam, and tears were streaming down the boy's face, shining, mixing with spit, as if he were bedewed with pearls. She leaped up off the chair and ran over to him, trying to push her hands under the animal's heavy carcass.

"Somebody's killed him . . ." whimpered the boy, wrestling with her over the dead cat and shoving his nose into the dense fur. Brigita began to shake when she managed to wrench the animal from the boy's embrace.

"Go into the house!" she barked, so loudly that at first he flinched and stared at her with blank, bloodshot eyes, and then slowly turned to the terrace door and went in. She was left alone with the limp carcass in her arms, shocked and furious, unable to fathom who could have done such a thing. She went into the garden shed for a shovel, and then noticed a big plastic bag in the corner full of leaves and twigs. She grabbed it in one hand, juggling so as not to drop the cat in the other, and went on to the edge of the yard, which dropped steeply off to the river. She set the cat on the ground and shook the leaves and twigs from the bag. Crumbles of tiny dried slivers flew up in the air and got under her clothes and into her nose while she first pushed the head into the bag, then bent the back, breaking it, and, in the end, tucked in the stiffened paws. The bag tumbled down the slope after the twigs and leaves, and after some five feet it snagged on something. She tried to reach it with her foot to kick it off, but when she realized she wouldn't be able to, she turned to look for help. There were no branches left, but her eyes were caught by the flower beds, edged with round white stones. She picked up the largest and from close up, winding her arm, she hit the plastic bag. Some ten seconds later, there was a light *splosh*, and nothing more to be seen. Brigita stood up and brushed the dust off, spitting:

"That shithead—what a fucking monster." Just then her cell phone rang, and the secretary announced, her voice trembling:

"Mrs. Arsovska, I am calling to inform you of a tragic event"—and then she burst into tears. Brigita waited patiently at the other end of the line for the secretary to pull herself together.

15.

Hunger

hunger steals my touch
hunger steals my soul

now (fall 2010)

"You're back! And the article is in my inbox," the editor declared by way of a greeting. Nora instinctively moved her cell phone away from her ear with a deep sigh.

"And hello to you, too," she greeted him politely, and then went on so he wouldn't have a chance to launch into one of his sermons: "You won't believe what just happened! This morning! I'm right on the spot; the press conference will be within the hour, or two at the most."

"Nora, what are you talking about? Where are you? You cannot still be there! You'd have made it back from Beirut by now. Send the article in immediately; we're in layout tomorrow."

"The mayor's been murdered." Here she paused for effect, and when she could tell she had his attention, she went on:

"Last night or early this morning. No public statement yet." She raced through the words.

"What? Did I hear you correctly? You're there?" She could hear the adrenaline surging through him at the breaking news.

"Yes, you heard me. I'm doing what I can to connect the dots." Then, surprising herself, she added: "I can do this." For a time, all she heard was silence; she could hear his brain working, the gears spinning.

"Oh fuck, fuck, fuck . . ." He seldom swore—only when he was at a total loss for a pithy, snide comment. "Fine, follow this through. Write down, word for word, everything you're hearing and send it in."

She made an effort to sound collected and professional. "As soon as I have something, I'll be in touch."

"So what's up with our Anna Karenina?" Her editor sometimes liked sounding smarter than he actually was.

"Almost done. I have a meeting with the ex-principal, and then I'll wrap it up. There you go. I'll ask her about the mayor, too, given their history . . ."

He interrupted: "I'll expect that this evening . . . By the latest tomorrow morning, with ribbons and a bow."

"I'll be in touch," she answered.

"I'll be waiting."

When she'd hung up, she decided not to think about her Anna Karenina who wasn't an Anna Karenina. Instead she wondered whether she should text Ms. Arsovska to remind her of their date, or simply keep to their agreement and head over to the Hotel Lav and wait for her. She decided it would be better not to text, which might give the ex-principal an opening to put off the meeting yet again. She left the eerily empty hotel lobby and stepped into the chill morning fog. In the distance, where the Vuka flowed into the Danube, was a large white stone cross that appeared ghostlike. Unable to take her eyes off it, she mused on the dense network of symbols you trek through in a life. If you don't read them correctly, any step you take may be the wrong one—and, depending on how rigid is the society you live in, it might be your last. Actually, you are best off mastering the language of symbols to perfection. Otherwise, if you know them only intuitively and avoid considering their deeper meanings, simply embracing the symbols as reality, you'll end up hoping against hope that the trek will turn out well. Intuitives, simpletons. On the other hand, if you know your symbols you can manipulate them—and also manipulate the people who run on instinct, using both as your weapons. The least useful is if you are cognizant of the symbols' profound irrationality and work to expose them, without recognizing their value over time, or the sheer violence they have acquired. Turning away from the cross, she glanced at the red brick of several nearby apartment buildings, the area where Marko had said he lived. She imagined him in bed. Her thoughts were involuntary, just images taking shape in her mind without prompting. Marko was waking and moving around in bed, the sheets were white—"What is wrong with you?" she muttered to herself, and rummaged for the pack of cigarettes in her purse. On the surface the city still looked the same; nothing had changed since the night before. The only difference was that the city was at its most animated in the morning, particularly around the outdoor market, where the average age of the people breathing life into it was about sixty. She decided to take a walk and kill the half hour left before her appointment. She tugged the sleeves of her jacket over her hands. Her skin felt taut and dry. The last few years she'd been suffering from an unusual allergy: whenever there was a sudden change in temperature, whether from hot to cold or vice versa, all the exposed parts of her body reddened and itched unbearably. Simply put, her immune system was unable to adjust to sudden temperature changes, and she had no idea why. Her organism was attacking itself so it wouldn't attack someone else: this was what she'd once read on the subject. She could tell that pale-red blotches were creeping across her face, and there was nothing she could do. She slipped through the crowd around the market tables of green stone and watched the faces of people who were closely examining the fruits and vegetables. She studied each face and couldn't help playing her private game: subtract twenty years and reconstruct their lives. She imagined these same faces and the hands—picking through the peppers and lifting the tomatoes for a sniff—clenched in terror, or covering their ears; she saw people fleeing in panic, or pointing a finger, or toting a weapon, or raising their hands to cover their eyes. She stopped in front of a stand selling grapes— so dark they were almost black; small, but not thick-skinned. Her fingers of their own accord reached for one and popped it into her mouth. The juice was sweet, fragrant, as if it had grown in some other soil. Then a voice startled her.

"I don't have much; I bring it along and if it doesn't sell, at least I'm out and about with other folks," said a man with gnarly hands like grape vines. "Take it, go ahead; you needn't pay me if you're just passing through." His voice was in total contradiction to his appearance, pure and soft, almost shining. Nora looked at him for a long time, then asked for two pounds . . .

no, four. He picked up a paper bag, and only then did Nora see the bad tremor in his hands; the grapes that spilled over when he tried to shovel them into the bag. His eyes were watery, as if about to pour out of their sockets. She didn't have to imagine him. She looked down at the ground. This part of town was the only part of the city that had been renovated after the city was "liberated." The rest lay in rubble for years, as if the authorities were afraid to rebuild what had been ravaged this way, so the marketplace area shone in contrast to the rubble. She'd seen the photographs: yellow façades, kitschy brick, red roof tiles, straight out of "Hansel and Gretel." Soon after peaceful reintegration, word got out that there was yet another mass grave right there under the marketplace. They tore the whole place down again. Undoubtedly there were bits and pieces still down there, gold-chain necklaces and the like. The grapes rolled off over the ground, and when she stepped on one, it squished and went from black to red. Nora took the paper bag, overpaid, and thrust in her fingers. She scooped grapes into her mouth, closed her eyes. As soon as she turned the nearest corner, she tossed the rest into a trash can.

16.

People from the cities

blue light on blue faces
and a blue voice from the blue box

now (fall 2010)

He hadn't slept in twenty-four hours. They'd roused him the night before around midnight, summoned him to the station just as he was starting to drive home, figuring that with so little traffic he'd be in bed in twenty minutes max. At the edge of town he swerved, cutting across double solid lines, and raced to Gundulićeva Street. His colleagues had secured the area and were holding anyone who might have seen something. A few tipsy kids had found the body. In a ditch, not far from the Serbian consulate, a man lay on his stomach, his face in the mud. They'd figured he was "dead drunk" when they spotted him stretched out like that and walked over to him, hooting and swigging booze. All they'd planned to take were his cigarettes; that's what they kept saying. Digging through his pants pockets and the inside of his jacket, they thought he was breathing. Using a cell phone as a flashlight, they saw that the mud on the man's temples was mixed with clotted blood. Then they panicked and fled, but the one who'd gotten blood on his hands decided it would be better to go to the police. The two others cursed his mother because they still weren't home when the police came knocking at their doors that night, and their shocked parents nearly fainted dead away. The police soon rounded up all three kids and brought them back to the scene of the crime to question them. Inspector Grgić arrived to find quite a crowd, so he parked at the entrance to the consulate. There were clusters of people scattered throughout the courtyard, like dark magpies descending on a meadow. Death was nothing new in the city, but it was associated more often with massacres than with this sort of intimate affair; people found this variety more difficult. About a hundred feet away, across the road, stood a group of his colleagues led by the coroner. A little farther on, the father of one of the boys who'd found the body was having a heated dispute with a policeman, with allusions to an attorney and trauma. Grgić, without a word of greeting, addressing his colleagues with only a nod, strode over to the ditch and crouched by the lifeless body. A small spotlight shone on the bloody hair and the pale, mud-splattered face of Nikola Vrcić, junior reporter. There were gobs of saliva and half-digested food around his mouth, and his right arm, though still attached to his body, looked as if it weren't his, or as if somebody had slapped it on as an afterthought, backwards, to his shoulder. Even a quick glance showed the death had been violent, but the cause wasn't easy to pinpoint. A nasty blow to the head, bloodstains on the pale concrete of the freshly laid curb some five feet from the ditch, the battered body and probably a fractured arm. Traces of vomit on the face. Once the larger spotlights were set up, they could see skid marks. The inspector paced slowly around the scene of the crime, making larger and larger concentric circles and checking the night sky more often. It was dark and pierced by stars, at once clear and black, as deep autumnal nights sometimes are. Steam rose from his nostrils and mingled with the smoke from the cigarette he'd pinned between his fingers. He wasn't supposed to be here at all; he should have left years ago. He'd seen everything at least once before—time was all that was needed for it all to be revealed. Over the last five years that Grgić had worked in the city, he wasn't living, or rather, sleeping, here—if, indeed, he ever slept. His home was in a small town some fifteen miles away, where he'd moved after his divorce and his training in Zagreb. He'd spent the war attending high school in Germany and stayed on there for a time to avoid serving in the army, then he returned and enrolled, in the early 2000s, in a two-year course in forensic science. At the time he never figured he'd always be moving within the same circle of people, and that half the time he'd be on the other side of the law in order to be complete and functional. He jailed petty dealers, gamblers, the occasional pedophile or rapist, but, alone, he couldn't break through the glass ceiling. To find a colleague who was willing not to take the line of least resistance was nearly impossible. The big fish he wanted and needed to lock up, the ones who had constructed and poisoned the system, were most often the very same people who, after he'd wrapped up an investigation successfully, decorated him with medals and meted out the praise. He had been following what was going over the last months in the city among the local powermongers; he'd followed the preparations for the privatization of the port, the games around bribery and the recording of the mayor, the appearance of a suspicious Romanian investor Ilinčić was pushing. The criminal activity fostered by the city leaders within the legal system was unfolding precisely as described in Criminal Organizations 101. Grgić knew he'd never make any headway if he attempted to clean up the criminality within the municipal ranks, but he was deeply aware nonetheless of what was going on around him. In that context, the violent death of the junior reporter looked to him like a private settling of accounts, if indeed it was deliberate, though he could already guess where the media speculation would go with this. Before he decided on any firmer conclusion, he glanced once more at the motionless body before he turned to walk back to the building of the consulate. In the reading room, on one of the chairs upholstered in green velvet, sat Velimirović, hunched over, his cell phone on his ear and his back to the door. The inspector stopped before entering and waited for Velimirović to finish, while straining to catch as much as he could of the conversation.

"Oh, yes, serious. Yes, yes. Very young . . . thirty-two . . . Look, the police are outside. We'll insist on an in-depth investigation . . . Yes. Two weeks ago . . . He received letters. Sure . . ." He glanced over his shoulder, and when he spotted Inspector Grgić he abruptly cut short the conversation, communicating with him already with his eyes.

"Call you later. Bye."

"Good evening," Grgić greeted him as he stepped into the room and swept it with a glance.

"Not a good evening." Velimirović rose from the chair, glowering.

"You're right, not so good." They both were silent for a moment, and then Grgić asked: "The two of you were together this evening?"

"Yes we were, as you've probably heard. There was a poetry reading here, and when it ended, people began to disperse, and Nikola came over to say goodbye, saying he'd go out and catch the poet to set a time tomorrow for an interview. It must have been an hour after that when the police came in and said some kids found him in a nearby ditch." He stopped for a moment and then went on: "He didn't get there by himself."

"So do you suspect anybody?"

"You know our situation," he said, trying to push things in that direction, just as Grgić had predicted.

"Yes? What situation? Would you be more specific?"

"Nikola was very active in the arena of minority rights, our local paper and so forth, and you can see for yourself what's going on in town, how they're smashing the signs, inflaming passions . . ." It was almost magnificent to observe Velimirović up close while he was doing what he did best.

"You're suggesting that a person motivated by nationalism killed him?"

"I am not suggesting anything," Velimirović suddenly hedged, throwing his hands in the air. "I'm just saying we mustn't ignore what has been going on here recently."

"Clearly," confirmed Grgić, going along with Velimirović's game. "The two of you were close? Had he ever let on that somebody wished him harm?"

"There are plenty of bad people around," Velimirović started saying, and then, suddenly, for the first time that evening, he remembered Nikola's cell phone, which would end up, most likely, in the hands of the police, if it hadn't already, and the messages they'd exchanged, and he broke out in a cold sweat. He knew he wasn't listed on the phone under his real name, but it wouldn't be difficult for someone to find their way to him if that was what they were after. Grgić immediately noticed the change in Velimirović's demeanor, though even he couldn't have guessed what had alarmed Velimirović. They'd been cautious, but nobody could have imagined that one of them would end up in a ditch. The last message sent had been about the previous night they'd spent in Nikola's apartment.

"Do you have anything more to ask, or . . ." asked Velimirović, ashen.

"Not for now. I'll have a word with the people outside, but we might summon you in the next few days to come down to the station and give another statement." Velimirović nodded absently. Gray figures were still pecking about in the yard; they would have dispersed—by then it was after one o'clock in the morning—but the police wouldn't let them leave. Grgić had gotten nothing more from them than statements like the one given by the woman who'd moderated the poetry reading: *He followed the poet out and didn't come back in.* After the final investigation he went to the station to put the papers in order. He was done by three in the morning, and then dropped off to sleep in an office armchair. He was woken by a colleague who shook him by the shoulder. The day was dawning.

"Up off your ass. The mayor's been murdered." He thought he must be dreaming; he didn't know where he was. He leaped to his feet. "Oh, fuck this life; everyone has gone crazy!" He splashed himself with water in the men's room and then went out to see yet another corpse, and then he grabbed a cup of coffee before he'd give the single sentence at the press conference that applied to both: "No comment at present; our investigation is underway."

17.

The ghetto

fog combs a lock of hair on the street
a cold breath from the west

now (fall 2010)

Every morning he bought four editions of the dailies in the two alphabets; he'd get into his car, drive to the bus station; sometimes he'd have an espresso at the counter in the bistro, and then he'd read the papers till noon if there were no customers. At this time of year the city was a mecca for cemetery tourism. Retirees, groups of hungover soccer fans, nursery-school children who were brought here in training to become society's future victims, professional patriots, foreigners: every fall they came pouring into the city to visit the massacre sites. They sniffed the air as if expecting to smell the blood, surveyed the lay of the land to gauge what the topographical difference was between an ordinary meadow and a mass grave, scowled with suspicion at the greenery of the grass, examined spots where the ground was bare. On their faces one could read gratitude for their own better fortune, mingling with the excitement of observing without participating. With a gasp they saw the geometrically arranged white stone crosses planted in the green grass as in American movies, and like mesmerized children they shook their heads in awe, admonishing one another with wagging fingers and umbrellas, reading aloud from the memorial plaque: *the youngest victim was six months old, the oldest one hundred and three; a pregnant woman was shot in the belly, shot in the belly . . . in the belly, uh . . .* rang out like an echo reverberating from the wobbly double chins and waterproof rainjackets purchased for just such excursions. At first he drove his taxi from mass grave to mass grave but refused to take tours to the pit. Until one morning when he spotted two young women speaking in English at the bus station. This was just when the site of the pit was being turned into a war memorial, and when Marko had only twenty kunas to his name. He needed another thirty if he was going to tank up on gas. The place was on his mind every day, and he knew he would have to go back there sooner or later. He went over to the women and inquired, discreetly, if they needed a lift. One of them didn't understand his question, presumably a foreigner, while the other said yes and asked how far to the pit. When he heard this he shook his head, thinking to beg off, but there was something in her eyes—something elusively dark and dry, so lost that it couldn't be more lost, something which gave him the feeling that he owed her and himself the trip to the pit. He sensed there was something that bound the young woman to that place, even if she'd never been there; he sensed that everything in the world depended on her going there. He could tell that it had to be him, that the moment had come.

"If you have thirty kunas, I'll take you. I'll have to stop at a gas station along the way," he said, eyes fixed on the ground. The woman took out a fifty and pushed it into his fist without waiting for change. Her foreign companion merely followed the transaction with animated eyes, only intuiting that something serious was going on here, such as, for instance, that somebody from the family of a person who had possibly been a victim at the pit was paying someone who had possibly been an executioner, a former reservist, to take her there. Not knowing, observing the taxi driver's attempt to redeem himself while knowing there was no way he could. When they got out of the taxi at the makeshift parking area, he stayed in the car, indicating with a glance that he'd wait for them. They walked away to a spot about a hundred feet from where he was parked. He watched the back of the foreign woman in her green jacket and stole glances at the face of the other woman. Between the two of them were about three feet of dirt and 250 dead bodies. The face of the young woman shattered into a thousand pieces while she shrugged her shoulders, doing what she could to answer questions in foreign words about something that couldn't be explained in her own words. Through the clouded windshield he could see in her eyes a pit filled with embarrassment and the desire to get through this as soon as possible. He froze that image in his mind, and in a ritual that night before he fell asleep he hammered it into the inside surfaces of his eyelids.

That morning he went right by the newsstand near his building without buying the papers, passed his car, and walked on into the center of town. He hoped he'd run into Nora somewhere; he wanted to call her, though he knew he never would. It had taken less than twenty-four hours for her face to start appearing before him no matter where he looked. He stopped at a newsstand in the center of town to buy his papers.

"Yes, neighbor?" asked the vendor with her frizzled yellow hair, peering out through the little window and looking at him only briefly. He piled up the papers and slapped down what he owed her without a word; she went on drawing him into conversation.

"We'll still be reading about this nightmare tomorrow. Who knows what really happened, and what the reporters will cook up next." She gave him a conspiratorial look, and this caught his attention.

"What?" he asked, to be polite.

"What? Where have you been living?" she shot back in an almost scornful tone, a little hurt that only now was Marko interested in the important information she had to impart.

"I'm not up on the news, neighbor, what happened?"

"The mayor's been murdered, that's what happened. No normal life for us here." She wagged her head, aware of her importance as the person with the breaking news.

Marko stared at her, incredulous. "When?" he asked, joining the conversation—something he almost never did.

"Last night. And a junior reporter was killed too. They'll be coming after us, one by one . . . No normal life for us . . ." The vendor repeated her mantra.

"Thanks." Marko picked up his newspapers and went on toward the pedestrian zone.

He sat on the terrace across the street from the café where he and Nora had spent the evening. Only then did he notice that there were more police in the city than usual. The day was cool, so he was the only customer sitting outside on the damp, bare chairs; the waiters hadn't yet put out the cushions. He logged on to the Internet sites of the newspapers, where he learned no more than he'd heard at the newsstand, but he was almost certain that Nora was still here for now. He went a few times into the list of contacts on his phone and the same number of times out of it, downed his coffee in a gulp, shot to his feet, and strode off toward his car, which he'd left parked by his building. *All this will pass* drummed in his head. What mattered was to feel nothing, and if he did feel something, to do nothing, because all this will pass, regardless. He walked mechanically through the streets and reached his car in three minutes, and in another two he was at the bus station. The bus was just pulling up, and there was always somebody who needed to be driven to somewhere on the outskirts of town, because city buses were infrequent. He was lucky and picked up a retired couple whom he drove, for the cost of two bus tickets, to an outlying village. He didn't make any money from the fare, but at least he was on the move. At least, while listening to them, he could evade his own thoughts. Docile, toothless old folks who didn't have much time left—but that didn't keep them from quarreling hotly over their opinions. He glanced a few times at the rearview mirror as they squabbled loudly, each looking out their window. Clearly they'd spent their life together and no longer had the need to look at each other.

"Well, for him, I'm telling you," insisted the granddad.

"I doubt it." The granny was unwavering.

"Where the hell did he get a house that size? Come on, you tell me," he pressed.

"He earned it; did he go off to Germany to work, or what?"

"Earned it my foot. They're all saying he worked at whatever;

if he'd gone to Germany he'd still be there. They wouldn't have locked him up. No, he smuggled people. And children." The granddad was exposing the head of the village, who'd just been locked up.

"Well, a person's got to make a living, what things you . . ." Granny wouldn't allow anything to tarnish her picture of the world, or the image of her neighbor who had a big house, three tractors, and embroidered curtains on the windows. People always had to have something to cling to. Marko didn't know whether he was struggling more with his thoughts or with the two of them and their vision of the world. When he finally left them out in front of a gray, unplastered house, he went to the gas station on the edge of the city. While he was paying, out of the corner of his eye he caught sight of a man at the other cash register whose face he wasn't sure if he was seeing or not, because since the night before, the past had begun pouring in through all the holes in his subconscious, and all the dams were giving way. Only when the heavyset, smooth-shaven man, more or less his age, gazed for a moment longer than necessary at Marko's face did he remember with a quiet chill the unopened bottle of whisky, and the life he'd saved so it could go on wreaking havoc.

18.

Room

in an empty room someone's things
dirty love in stains

now (fall 2010)

After the first terse sentence Inspector Grgić gave the journalists in the hotel foyer, telling them there'd be no information or statements regarding the murders, the grumbling of the dissatisfied locals and two or three bigshots from national television spread through the room, just as he'd anticipated. He gestured to them to let him continue.

"We understand the public would like to know what has happened, and they have the right to be informed. We have called you here to tell you whatever we can," he went on, shifting his weight in his chair.

Then he explained that because these were cases of special interest, he had the leeway to inform them of the victims' personal information, which would otherwise be held back from the public, and as soon as circumstances so allowed he would be doing just that. He filled in with phrases that said nothing, because there was nothing further to say. He confirmed that both the mayor and Nikola Vrcić, junior reporter, had been killed the night before. After being called in, the police had blocked access to the areas, and today there would be heightened surveillance of vehicles and drivers.

Traces taken from the places where the murders happened, both the mayor's apartment and the site where the body of the junior reporter was found, had been sent to the Center for Forensic Investigation, and findings were expected in the next hours or days. With the help of the findings they hoped to discover who had committed the murders, and then, perhaps, who might have ordered them.

"I can tell you that quite a large quantity of material evidence has been collected." He coughed significantly, knowing that his "quite a lot" had no basis whatsoever in reality. "We are waiting on the forensics. Everything suggests that what happened here was a complex act, requiring a complex investigation," said Grgić and added that the investigation was now in the purview of the county attorney's office, and he was confident the cases would be solved.

Sitting in the front row, Nora waved her hand in the air the whole time, and though he'd said at the outset that because of confidentiality concerns he would not be responding to questions from the press, as soon as he finished his last sentence and began putting papers into his briefcase, Nora spoke up in a loud, assertive voice.

"Can you at least say whether you suspect that the two murders might be linked in some way?" Grgić looked in her direction and said wearily: "Miss, you weren't listening to what we said at the beginning . . ."

"I was, but this truly is in the public interest." This time Nora was not backing down.

"For now we have no such indication," he said, using a textbook phrase, hoping in the same breath to express his thanks and sidestep any further discussion.

"Has anybody requested police protection?" She quickly jumped in again.

"There have been no requests for police protection." He punched each word, already irritated. The rest of them followed Nora's example, and the questions came raining down one after another. Someone who'd watched one too many episodes of *Midsomer Murders* mentioned "the perfect murder," which prompted thinly veiled irony in Grgić's voice. He explained that hypothetically every murder which has as its goal the death of the victim is perfect as far as motivation is concerned, but the police believe there is no such thing as a perfect murder. After this he rose abruptly to his feet, nodded, and hurried out of the foyer. The journalists soon began to disperse, and Nora looked around, hoping Brigita still might turn up, although by then it was reasonably clear that she wouldn't. Perhaps she'd known this already that morning; maybe she'd have left Nora in the lurch regardless. Soon Nora was alone; the room around her had emptied, the diligent waiters were already folding the chairs. Her mind was working at a mile a minute, but she hadn't formed any conclusions. There was no obvious motive for either of the murders of the night before. A chill ran down her spine when she realized she'd been in the vicinity of the consulate just before the time of the murder, and somewhat later she'd been near the apartment of the murdered mayor. She rose slowly from her chair when she saw that the waiter was standing six feet from her, his arms discreetly crossed, waiting for her to get up so he could tidy the foyer. She decided to go back to her hotel room and take at least two hours to enter on her laptop all the reactions that were racing through her mind, and then arrange them in some sort of order that could help her organize her train of thought. She was taken with anxiety when she realized there were at least two separate files to think about—one for the schoolteacher and the other for the mayor. Although the first was her primary assignment and the reason she was here, she had almost no desire to go near it. But there was no way to avoid it; she'd have to take a deep breath and write what was expected of her. She walked back to the hotel, staring at the ground, concentrating on every detail she could remember having to do with the mayor's case. The port? Everyone knew he was a wreck after the recording had been made public, and furthermore was politically dead, though he kept trying to play the victim. So why kill him physically as well? He no longer had any sway or power. On the other hand, at least according to what she'd been able find out, the murder was committed far too professionally for it to be a crime of passion. Those crimes were almost always gory and messy, and were the work of those closest to the murder victim. In them there was always love which had turned to hate. They weren't deliberate, just as love itself is never deliberate, and that was why the killer always left such a mess behind, and why the people or things around them suffered the consequences. Occupied with those thoughts, she reached her room, but as she entered she took a step back to check on the brass number affixed to the doorframe. This must be the wrong room. She didn't spot her things on the table and chair; they weren't where she'd left them. When she'd made sense, after a couple of seconds, of what she was looking at, and when she saw that the number on her key and the number on the door were one and the same, she realized somebody had been there. Somebody had definitely been in her room. Someone had smashed the chair, overturned the desk, pushed one of the beds over, and flipped the other over on its side. Nora's clothes were flung around the room, tossed over the bed and window, over the cupboard door, and on the floor. She reached for her things, but as she picked up each item of clothing, it fell to pieces. The sleeve fell off her T-shirt, the legs off her pants; all of her clothes had been sliced up with scissors and left in heaps of scraps. Then she froze, midroom, when she remembered her laptop. She couldn't even tell where to turn to look for it. She'd left it on the bed, under the blanket, but the blankets were on the floor and the beds were laid bare. It was gone. She broke out in a cold sweat and was paralyzed by fear. Walking backwards, she slowly left the room. She closed and locked the door and then ran down to the front desk. Nobody was there; the only sound was the radio softly humming, shattering the silence.

"Hello!" she shouted nervously, leaning over the counter. No response.

"Hello!" she called even louder, and from the depth of the dark corners of the hotel appeared the receptionist-waiter.

"Yes, Miss, where's the fire?" he asked with a prim smile.

"Somebody broke into my room and stole my laptop; all my things have been thrown all over the place; who went up there?" she blurted out in a single breath.

"What? Impossible." The waiter shook his head, grinning, hyenalike, with his yellowed teeth.

"What do you mean, impossible? Go up yourself; it's as if a bomb went off in there! Somebody must have heard!" By now she was yelling.

"Calm down, everything will be fine; we'll resolve the misunderstanding. Slow down." For a moment Nora went mute, and he continued. "Perhaps you misplaced something; you came in late last night, perhaps you don't remember everything . . . and a small room can become messy in no time." The expression on his face was a mask of concern.

"I'll report this to the police. Please, I beg of you, don't let anybody go up there; I want the inspector to see it. I now have lost everything I need to do my job; do you understand me?" She had the impression that he didn't understand or was pretending not to. She dashed out of the hotel, running as fast as she could, and within two minutes she was out in front of the police station. Traffic had been blocked, and there was a crowd out in front. As she tried to push her way in, people were filming the uproar on their cell phones. She didn't have a chance to figure out what was going on, but out of the corner of her eye she noticed a policeman and a local person, arguing.

"Where are you going?" A man in a uniform stood in front of her, scowling and serious; he'd been watching her ever since she came running across the street.

"Please let me in, I need to report a robbery," she said in all seriousness, but the policeman didn't seem to be taking her seriously.

"You'll have to step away; apparently a protest without a permit is starting. Come back later."

"How can I come back later, whatever could you mean, my things, my laptop, they've all been stolen." She was on the verge of tears. The policeman slipped his arm through hers and led her to the back of the building. At the back entrance he asked for her first and last name.

"Nora Kirin," she answered, looking him straight in the eyes.

"Little Miss Kirin"—he leaned over to her ear—"if you go straight down there and then to the left, that's where the inspector is, and he just came in; be careful to tell him everything that happened." Then he paused, and added, even softer: "A laptop can be replaced. Other things not so easily, as you know so well." Then he turned and walked away, leaving her alone in the hallway. Nora froze. She thought of her mother, all the police stations where she'd waited in the corridor for her, her mother's face as they saw her out. She made her way to the inspector's office. The door was open, and he was not alone. She recognized the coat, the little purse, the lace: Melania Gmaz was sitting across from him. Nora stepped closer to the door so she could hear what they were saying.

"He threatened him; I saw it with my own eyes," Melania testified doggedly.

"He threatened the mayor," repeated the inspector as he took notes. "And can you repeat what it was, exactly, that he said to him?"

"That he fucked his mother, and he told the Chinese man that he fucked his mother, too, and that he'd knock him flat and that the fish in the Danube would eat him. Which isn't actually logical, is it." This last comment was for herself.

"What isn't logical?" he asked, confused.

"That he'd knock him flat and throw him into the Danube!" She shrugged and looked up, seeking help from above. She'd reported so many injustices and crimes by then that she knew there was little chance she'd be taken seriously, but after the murder of the mayor she knew she had to report what she'd seen. Ilinčić picking him up by the collar in the parking lot and threatening to kill him. She believed unwaveringly in the institution of civil duty—unlike Nora, who wised up that instant. She turned to the exit, realizing she'd been chased into a trap. Ever since her father had been killed, ever since her mother was never allowed to initiate an investigation, ever since, after nearly twenty years, she'd come home. She knew there was no way to handle this with kid gloves. She took a deep breath and steeled herself, this time, to deal with this differently. She took her cell phone from the back pocket of her pants, went into her contacts, and clicked on the letter M.

19.
Hey, Mama

hey, mama, what's your son doing
hey, mama, who is there with him?
hey, mama, fear for his life?
hey, mama, he's done wrong

now (fall 2010)

The barrier arm blocking access to the parking lot wasn't lifting; he began honking nervously so the guard, who as usual wasn't in his booth, would finally let him in to park by the national library in Belgrade. The morning light refracted from the crosses on the Church of Saint Sava, in the droplets of water spraying from the fountains around the church; it shone on the beggars and Gypsies, tourists and monks, on the smudged windows of the cars snaking through gridlock in the surrounding streets. Illuminated by surreal autumnal light, a morning that no longer felt like the day when he was to receive yet another literary prize, this one emanating from the warm embrace of novelist-cum-politician Dobrica Ćosić. These laudations had been easy to come by. His face was unshaven, the bags under his eyes reached down to his knees, and his eyelid twitched uncontrollably while he waited for the lowly creature in a gray uniform to come along and press the red button. He checked to see what his eyes looked like in the rearview mirror and saw red. The color of the previous night was black. Well, red at first, the red of the traffic sign with the white circle. Red announcing he shouldn't drive the wrong way down the one-way street; he drove into a side street that he thought would take him out to the main road and the hotel. Then came the color black, darkness, the moment when he shifted the car into reverse, having changed his mind, calculating he'd be better off ignoring the red traffic sign and driving down the street the wrong way anyway. There was nobody out, after all. He glanced back over his shoulder while driving forward. When he pressed his foot on the gas to traverse the short one-way street as quickly as possible, the Volvo gave a wild lurch, noise; no color then. A thud or a bump. Noisy and fleshy, and, he could tell, alive and so fragile. And tossed to the side. He stopped for a second; his heart almost vomited, the sounds of applause and the shrill women's voices still ringing in his ears. In panic he peered around. Should he get out and check? Suddenly sober. He thought of pulling it into the car and taking it to a forest somewhere nearer the border with Serbia. He considered the pits and water wells in adjacent villages. The Danube and the toothed carp. And how this would never occur to anybody. But death is contagious, and when he pictured the corpse in his car—first on the front seat; no, even worse, in the back; oh, definitely not in the trunk—he realized he couldn't. He wasn't that man. And then he thought tenderly of himself and his precious life, and again he pressed the gas. Godnar drove to the hotel in a total trance; later he had no recollection of the drive, that was the black, the hole that engulfed everything and left behind only fear for his skin or ass, depending. He swept up all his things from the room, found himself in the parking lot, and then remembered his ID card and almost shat himself while he waited at the front desk of the hotel for what seemed like an eternity, listening to the hollow instrumental music. He only came to while waiting in the access lane, a few hundred feet from the border with Serbia. He remembered he hadn't even examined the hood of his car up close to see if there was any damage. Luckily, the damage was minimal on such a big, sturdy chassis. For the first time in the last two hours he felt a welling of sincere joy and no trace of shame. He was only the tiniest bit sheepish about the very lack of shame he'd felt.

"Good evening," he said heartily while staring at the square-shaped light by the little gray box of a booth. The border policewoman didn't return his greetings. Without a word she took his documents and peered into his car. Her tired gaze danced from her screen to the plastic card and traffic permit, then returned them to him a few minutes later, and he slowly crossed the bridge, driving in second gear, holding his breath, and drove up to the next border agent. An even smaller metal booth, and as he slowed, a man's hairy arm was all that emerged and waved at him to pass. He nearly choked with joy.

Taking care to respect every single traffic regulation, driving every minute below sixty-five, he was in the Voždovac neighborhood of Belgrade within two hours, elated and trembling in his big, warm bed. He didn't feel at all as if he'd just killed a man and fled the scene. A man he'd hugged only hours before, promising him a big interview for the next issue of *Izbor*. As he commented in an aside about the icy reporter lady with the little, poetically brazen tits, he realized the *Izbor* reporter was gay, and this put him off slightly, but still he liked the man. The different things that happened the night before had nothing, as far as he was concerned, to do with each other. He felt no guilt. Indeed, he felt as if someone had given him a new lease on life. For two difficult hours he slept the sleep of the dead and woke up early, before dawn, while the chaotic city of Belgrade was bathed in gray-lilac murky light. At first he didn't think of all that had transpired; then he broke out in a cold sweat only a few minutes after waking. He jumped up and put water on for coffee, opened his laptop, and began scrolling for news. Nothing yet. He entered his name, and there wasn't even a word about the poetry reading. Maybe, after all, the man hadn't . . . He kept refreshing the page as morning dawned and then began readying to go and receive the award. He was wide awake by then, and reality had begun to sink in; he was queasy with fear of possible evidence. Having arrived too early, he first parked in the official lot of the library and then wandered the foyer, reading the posters on the bulletin board. Below his photograph and the announcement about the award ceremony there were notices of labor-union discounts available to library staff for the purchase of bedding and Zepter cookware. This seemed somehow pitiful, somehow tawdry, somehow unfair. He couldn't imagine why everything around him had suddenly gone so rapidly downhill, why people had no teeth or souls; there was something false in everything around him. That very thought momentarily appalled him. Like the many others who were wandering around with him, there was no mobility to his neck, and his gut was hard as a rock. He'd never stopped to look left or right, never back, only forward, *avanti*, ahead, straight into the fragmented stupidity which allowed no forward movement. He had no soft core, only a terrible, rigid, stonelike gut, preventing him from crouching, squatting, down to the point where everything begins. All he knew to do was to march onward, especially over those who couldn't stand, and from the heights he couldn't hear the joints snapping and the flesh rotting. He had no past, he knew nothing of it; all he had were images, until he simplified them to the point that they became comprehensible, ordinary, and comforting. Climbing the steps to the great hall, he stared at the thick, heavy curtains that had enshrined the vast windows for almost forty years, inscribed with writings from the gospels. He remembered his grandfather, Miroslav, and an incident when he and his grandfather had been traveling by train while he was still a very small boy. The train had stood for a whole eternity between Ruma and Šid when a woman poked her head into the compartment to ask whether they knew what had happened and why they were standing there so long. The old man said nothing at first, but when he exhaled a cloud of reeking smoke from his endless mouth, staring out the window, he simply said: *runover*. Without a blink. Things like that were always happening everywhere. Godnar strode into the hall; the people rose to their feet and applauded.

SP   SP   SP

The special session, open to the public, had been scheduled to start more than a half hour before. The journalists and camera operators were buzzing around in the hallways, and the deputy to the mayor who'd been killed the night before—more recognizable for being the only person in a gray suit than for anything else—was seeking, with his gaze, the support of at least some of the members of his political party on the council so he could call the session to order. Almost all of them, at least in the first rows, stared at the floor or straight ahead. In a shaky voice he called on those present to hold a moment of silence. The hall was filled with the noise of metal chair legs scraping on the parquet floor, until all the representatives were standing. The week before, when the mayor had shown up at a session unannounced, at the moment the municipal budget was voted down by one vote, they'd also averted their eyes. At the time he'd been on sick leave, waiting for the state attorney's office to initiate proceedings, and then he'd ended up having a surgical operation that was presented by the opposition as the most ordinary sort of excuse spun to the press. As the meeting was about to get underway, he'd come charging into the hall, tripping over the camera cables and microphones, and torn off his suit jacket. His voice had cracked as he unfastened the buttons on his shirt, ripped away the bandages and gauze with trembling fingers, and displayed the fresh scar from his recent heart operation, when he'd had a pacemaker implanted. There were sutures—as black as disease—protruding from the swelling, blistering skin, and to the council members, until only yesterday colleagues and friends, he'd offered to pull his heart from his body so as to cut short the speculation in the media about him feigning illness. Ashen and rumpled, he'd glared straight at Brigita, who was sitting in the first row, while she fixed her gaze on the pile of papers before her. Soon after this performance, the decision was adopted to hold new elections, costing the city—with one of the highest rates of unemployment in the country—another thirty million kunas. Now again she fixed her gaze in front of her, while all she could see before her eyes were Darko's bare feet and the foam from the cat's snout dripping down them.

"Please take your seats," announced the mayor's deputy after a full minute of silence. Nobody needed to be asked to be quiet; they were all waiting for him to speak, in hopes that they wouldn't have to.

"First"—he coughed, visibly shaken and smoothing his thinning hair across his head toward his ears—"may I express my grief at this indescribable tragedy, and then my sympathies to the family, friends, and colleagues of our late mayor. I hope the police will do their job as quickly and efficiently as possible so we can bring stability back to the city." The councillors nodded in sympathy. The deputy paused, drumming his fingers on the table and swaying slightly in place, and did what he could to gain control over his voice. "Until then, we can't do much, can we, under these extraordinary circumstances. Over the next days we'll set the date for the new election, and until then technical matters will be handled as usual. Allow me to dissolve the council in its current form, and thank you all for your service." He nodded and sat back down. The councillors soon started fidgeting, turning to one another and whispering. None of them were in any hurry to vacate their positions, either literally or metaphorically, though judging by the recent developments and imminent election, it was inevitable that some of them would be leaving their seats on the council. Just as it was clear that what with the growing poverty and upsurge in nationalism, the next election, after a pause of only three years, would be won by a coalition of right-wing parties. At the same time a major drama was brewing among the representatives of the minorities, because the founders of ethnobusiness who'd reigned supreme for many, many years were finding themselves, for the first time, on unsure footing. Velimirović was still thriving at the national level, inching his way gradually toward the Croatian parliament on Saint Mark's Square in Zagreb, but among the locals there was growing discontent with the way in which he had represented their interests. The vast wealth he'd amassed over the last years was in inverse proportion to the despair and neglect of the surrounding, mainly Serbian, villages. Feelings ran especially high after rumors circulated that at his new wife's insistence he'd signed his own daughter up for school to follow the Croatian instead of the Serbian curriculum. Better that the kid had two hours extra every week of French and piano, instead of Serbian language and culture classes. And besides, once Dad won his mandate as a deputy to the national assembly, she'd be attending secondary school and university in Zagreb. And it wouldn't do for her to be so far behind her peers in school. What was the point of learning about the Battle of Kosovo, anyway? Velimirović could only agree, while in public he continued fiercely to defend the model of ghetto schooling by which the children of Serbian nationality were taught according to the curriculum used in Serbia. He was constantly raising a ruckus about how parents, under threat to do so or by taking the easy way out, were forcing their children to assimilate as if they were the new kids on the block. Privately, he knew full well that children who'd gone through the Serbian school system while living in Croatia would not have equal opportunities, but he successfully bartered with peoples' emotions, drives, and myths, as much as the situation allowed. The voices against him were growing more determined, and he had his eye on Councillor Arsovska more often now, greeting her with courtesy in the hallways. He was waiting for the right moment to approach her.

"No need to feel awkward," he said softly after the final session, approaching her from behind and brushing her elbow in passing.

"Pardon?" Sincerely surprised, Brigita turned to Velimirović.

"Oh, you know, I meant about all this." He knew she was a savvy woman, but he was wondering whether she'd feign ineptitude, and to what degree. Many eyes were on her; the mayor's dizzying plummet had followed after her report, and word had it that she'd destroyed the man's life by recording him, when all the rest of them were doing the same things, the only difference being that there were no recordings of their dealings.

"I'm not feeling awkward at all, don't worry; I feel sorry for him, like everybody else does. That I reported him for bribery has nothing to do with all this," she said, looking him straight in the eyes.

"Of course it doesn't; I didn't mean to insinuate, I just want you to know you have my support." He was being discreet and equivocal.

"Thank you for that." Her first thought was to shrug him off politely, but then suddenly this didn't seem so useless and pointless, the support he was allegedly offering. Even if her party were to win the election, their victory would probably be a close one, and every hand would be welcome. Far too fresh in memory was the way her party had been savaged for its transformation into a criminal organization brandishing the red-and-white checkerboard flag, its far-reaching devastation of the economy, the thefts of unheard-of magnitude under the banner of social welfare. On the other hand, also fresh in her memory was the former prime minister, currently in prison, who, the Christmas before last, when he found the special coin in his mouthful of the traditional bread served at Serbian Christmas, shouted the Serbian Christmas greeting, "Christ is born!"—a rare move of his that was not a disgrace. And if he could make that concession, maybe this here wasn't so unimaginable.

"Now there will be chaos; who knows how long this situation will last . . ."

"Yes, I hope everyone will be reasonable; that would be in everyone's interest." They uttered these hollow phrases while looking at each other, eyes shining. At that moment, in the spheres of the unsaid a new coalition was born, formed based on a pure, unsullied hunger for power. While wrapping up the formalities, Brigita spotted a young woman who was staring at her intently, standing by the door. She assumed this must be the journalist she'd said she'd meet. She'd have to walk right by her; no longer could this be avoided. She went over to her, and before Nora had a chance to say a word, Brigita said:

"Please don't be offended; I know I promised to talk with you, but as you can see, so much has happened in the meanwhile, that simply isn't possible now." The decisive tone in her voice was firm.

"So I thought," nodded Nora, looking deep into her and unsettling Brigita's poise.

"Sorry, I'm really in a hurry." She tried to slip by Nora, who hadn't budged. "Will you let me pass?" Brigita was getting nervous.

"Will you tell me what you know?" She answered the question with a question.

"Young lady, I know what everyone else knows; please, find someone else," she almost snapped at her. At that moment Velimirović came over, introducing even denser and more suffocating air to the space among the three.

"Oh, you're here, too," he said to Nora. She merely nodded, clutching her cell phone in hand.

"Come now, no need for this to be awkward; you are very unprofessional." Brigita was visibly irate at Nora's stubborn blocking of the door, keeping her from passing.

"Well, I guess you all are professionals." Nora enunciated slowly, looking at Brigita and then at Velimirović. "You've always been professionals," she said.

"Hey, get Zvonko; we have a problem here at the door." Brigita called to the deputy to summon security.

"No problem." Nora stepped back with a smile. "No need. We'll be professional; thank you, Zvonko," she said to the man twice her size who was lumbering her way. She turned and went out into the street. Her cell phone almost fell from her hand as she sprinted to the hotel.

20.

Synchro

I came to carry you
to the homes of my ancestors
to tell you there is no night
you should give up
desire is hunger is fire

now (fall 2010)

A young nun was sitting on a stool out by the entrance to the general hospital, strumming a guitar. *The Messiah will come.* In front of her stood two more nuns, thrilling aggressively to God's mercy. With them in their circle were a dozen middle-aged women, hopping from foot to foot with the cold, and a man in a public works uniform who was going from one to the next, offering them chocolates from a box. They took the chocolates, but since they were singing and being filmed for a local TV crew, they didn't put the chocolates into their mouths but instead held them behind their backs until they melted in their fingers. Later they licked their fingers on the sly. Up on the second floor, closer to God, where the inharmonious strains of the poorly written songs, unrealistic hopes, and tacky melodies reached, was the ward for gynecology and obstetrics. Another man in the group outside, the leader of the national Initiative for Life, stepped forward, military style, and barked into his megaphone:

"And I am especially glad that your city has joined our initiative with the goal of forcing the hospital to cease offering abortions; we hope the mothers will understand that what they are carrying under their heart is alive, our brother or sister, and we love them and want them!" At this point applause erupted among those who were gathered, while only a dozen feet above them the ward's head nurse looked down at them and silently closed the window.

Nora was on her way back to the hotel from the assembly, back to the chaos of her room, holding her cell phone all the while. With no plan. An icy wind blasted her in the face. Wasn't there a kind of cake called "Icy Wind"? Her tears chilled her red cheeks and left dark tracks down them. She did the only thing she could do on such a day and the first thing she'd wanted to do as soon as she woke up.

"Hello?" He sounded as if he'd been watching his cell phone the whole time.

"Hey, hi. Nora here. Sorry to bother you." She couldn't come up with anything better.

"Are you okay?" he interrupted, concerned.

"Well, not really, but well, maybe I'll leave here today . . . I don't know, they stole my laptop." She spoke jerkily, trying to sound almost cheery while there was a lump rolling around in her throat, as she tried to smile, hating the corners of her mouth as they kept slipping downwards.

"Nora, tell me, where are you?" His voice was firm and calm.

"I'm here by the hospital; I'm watching them pray on their rosaries for the unborn brothers and sisters." She meant to sound sarcastic, just to change the subject.

"Wait there, please, one minute. Okay?"

"Fine," she said softly and swallowed a mountain. Shouts reached her.

"And one more thing," declared the leader, inspired by the Holy Spirit, feeling the traditional Christian anguish of persecution after the nurse closed the window. "I am particularly moved to see you gathered here, brothers and sisters, in this very city that during Yugoslavia was the main center for the deliberate termination of pregnancies. Parents from all parts of the country came here to abort their children. Many have said that the horrors of the war are a direct consequence of that sad reality."

Visible on the faces of those gathered was approval for this terrible and logical notion, mixed with cloying horror.

"The Initiative for Life will bring the great light of hope to this people; every act of goodness is returned in kind." Nora felt as if she were watching them from another planet. She hoped the curses of the devout hadn't reach the second floor, blaming women for wars, for all the evils of the world, the plagues of locusts and everything the good Lord God would soon be raining down upon us. Again the strains rang out of the hollow melodies, destroying the very meaning of music and prayer, without a shred of understanding or talent for life, born or unborn. The white Corsa pulled over to the side of the road, and Marko opened the door and did what he could to catch Nora's eye. She sat in the passenger seat, staring in front of her, terrified by what would happen once their eyes met. When she muffled the sounds by shutting the door, she dropped her head and her hair slid over her cheeks, hiding the blush that was climbing up her throat, impinging on her chin, ears, and cheekbones. Marko turned toward her, waiting for the curtains to rise. She rubbed her face and pushed aside her hair, and then she dropped her hands into her lap, staring at the red backs of her hands on her knees. He reached over to her chin and slowly turned her face to him. With his thumbs he smoothed away the traces of the black, salt-strewn streets under her eyes, erased all the pavement and potholes, brought back the woods. The moment she looked at him everything was flooded, the bridges and city, the devastated buildings and the bones deep underground; the interior of the car gradually filled with water, the houses were inundated, the red roof tiles floated up and away on the green surface of the river with those green eyes. When he released her after an entire eternity from his arms, the waters ebbed, leaving behind things, thousands and thousands of small and large things along the shore tangled up in the bare branches that were still hanging menacingly over them. Nora wiped her face with a tissue, and Marko said:

"Let's go."

"Where?" she asked without any anxiety.

"To pick up your things at the hotel."

Nora nodded and buckled her seatbelt.

⁍   ⁍   ⁍

Just a couple of years for us
it swells like hope, like sea, like speech
like movement, like dawn, like child, like blood
like desire between us
it swells like pain
and gnaws everything before our eyes
love me like you've never loved

"Come in." He unlocked the door and pointed her toward the small hallway. The space was unexpectedly light and orderly, full of wooden bookshelves with books and CD holders. The apartment had two small rooms; the hall led into the living room and then the dining area, which was next to the kitchen. The walls were white, except one, light green, which separated the living room from the bedroom. On it were posters by Danijel Žeželj; that was all. Marko set Nora's backpack down in the hall, took her coat, and pointed her toward the dining-room table with two chairs.

"Sit down; I'll make us some coffee." He ducked behind the kitchen wall, and Nora had a look around the room. She felt comfortable; there was nothing superfluous. Warm colors and straight lines. On the table was a book, open, facedown. She picked it up.

Beasts love the fatherland
Beasts are the real liberators, unsurpassed revolutionaries
Beasts give the last drop of their blood
for the fatherland
Beasts howl until they are hoarse for the fatherland
Beasts claw at you, dig in talons, rip open throats

if you didn't carry the flag you're in for a dead man's shroud
Beasts suck out your blood if you aren't in the chorus, in the first
   trench
As soon as war breaks out beasts blow up
moral, law, conscience
Beasts know god forgives them all they do
Beasts love the fatherland and serve it loyally
Beasts are holy liberators
So for their reward they seek all the power and all the wealth.

She put down the book. The words took her to pieces inside and then put her back together again.

"Milk?"

Marko peered around the wall.

"Hmmm?" It wasn't easy for her to make her way back.

"Milk?" he asked.

"This poetry is amazing." She looked at him, glassy-eyed. Marko frowned, and then he realized she was referring to the book on the table.

"Ah—Idrizi, a Kosovar poet; brilliant," he said with respect.

"Where do you get books like this?" asked Nora.

"Well . . . there are people I talk to. Not many, they'd all fit on one bus, but luckily there are a few. If you like . . . take it, I'll get another copy."

"Yes, yes, to decontaminate from last night's reading." Nora smiled.

"Oh, yes, that was definitely hard-core," he agreed. "But, milk?" He smiled.

"Sure, sure . . ."

Soon he appeared with two cups, set one down in front of

her, and took the other seat. The afternoon was quiet, as if somebody had withdrawn all the sounds from the room except for the soft sound of Chet Baker's trumpet coming from Marko's laptop—but that sound was distinct, separate from all others. It didn't disturb the silence. For a time they sipped their coffee, exchanging occasional glances.

"Will you tell me what happened?" he said, finally. For a time she was quiet.

"Uh, I don't know where to begin." She knew exactly what he was asking of her, but she still hadn't told anyone what happened, and everything was linked to everything else. It always is; nothing ever starts with now. It never starts with one event; there is no cause and effect, there is cause, cause, cause, and a few more times like that, and then effect. And then again. And that deeper logic that governs things, that brought them to this quiet room for confessions.

"Okay," she said and pulled her hair scrunchy off her wrist. She drew her hair into a ponytail, sat up straight, and planted her elbows on the table. She ran her fingers over the edges of the volume of poetry. She looked at him sideways.

"My father was murdered," she said for the first time. Marko nodded, saying nothing, letting her go on. "I never learned who did it to him or who ordered it; I know that some were involved who are still in power today, but there's no proof. I think Ilinčić was one. I think this is why he had my room turned upside down. I think they are all somehow embroiled in this and that there's no way to stand up to the alliance of all these criminals and the people in government. I think all this together has something to do with the mayor's murder, but I haven't been able to get to the bottom of how. I think they are all the same people." Her voice was muted and deep. "Mainly, I want to find out what happened. I want to know who it was." They looked at each other for a fraction of a second, as if the image had frozen, then blurred, and then sharpened again. Something was happening with space, time, air; something had begun to grow between them, like the sea, like dawn, and eroded everything before their eyes. Words fell short, but words were all they had just then.

"I'll tell you everything I know." Marko, too, was saying these words for the first time. He reached for his cigarettes on the table, but he didn't take them out, he just spun the pack in his fingers.

"I was a reservist. I was Velimirović's bodyguard," he said slowly, to the end, quiet and braced for any reaction. "I was at the pit when the massacre happened. I wanted to kill myself afterward. I didn't, but I was no longer alive. I was eighteen then, and I knew nothing about anything; I thought I'd save my mother, and I thought I was supposed to defend my homeland. Both of those things were illusions. I can't change that, unfortunately, and if I could, I'd trade places with the people who were killed that night . . . or with your father. If only I could." He looked at her, his eyes red; he didn't cover his face, he wept soundlessly. "Until now I've never found anyone I cared to tell these things to. Nobody with whom I'd be less alone. I know far too much." He took a deep breath and paused. Tears streamed down Nora's face. Everything was wrong. Marko went on.

"What I know about your father I overheard one evening during some so-called negotiations. Ilinčić was definitely one of the people who ordered it, and Velimirović and his crew were grateful to him for doing it. Nobody wanted to stop the war. See? Nobody who could have. He was killed by someone who was a kid like me. Washed out and fucked over. I didn't know that at the time, and I saved the kid's life; later he went right on doing more of the same . . . Killing. I saw him this morning in the city. It's likely that he has something to do with what happened last night, quite likely. There you have it." Nora dropped her head into her hands; her shoulders shook; in her thoughts surfaced the reptilian eyes and the cherry cordial, and a toast with the man who'd murdered her father. When she pulled herself together, they could look longer at each other for the first time. In the midst of the desert where they'd been sitting for years, each in isolation—roasting by day, whipped by frigid winds at night, in the middle of nowhere, hoping for nothing—now they'd met. Their hands were close, lying on the table, only inches apart, although those inches were the longest journey anyone had ever travelled. First he touched the joints of her fingers along the edge of her palm, and then he took her hand in his. The first touch in life.

༄ ༄ ༄

You are all my pain
you are all my pain
you are all my pain
you are all my pain
you are all my pain
you are all my pain
you are all my pain

She started awake in the middle of the night. The window curtains were parted, and a milky yellow light shone into the room; she couldn't remember right away where she was. To the left of her body the warmth hit her, and when she turned, she saw his sleeping face. Relaxed. Peaceful. Without deep creases and tightly pressed lips, nearly unrecognizable. Momentarily she remembered everything. How she was sitting in the chair and how he reached for her. How he sat on the bed and how she sat in his lap. How the colors in the room began to melt and how they talked, from the beginning. When they were twelve and the world was different, when the clouds were white and low, and when there was promise. And how the desert was deaf and endless, and how solitude became precious. Then they did everything, from the beginning, all for the first time, they grew up together while he squeezed her around the throat till she was dizzy and then kissed her, they threatened each other, growled, sobbed, hit, and then stroked all the bruises with reverence. For hours. Nothing held back; they recast all the familiar words, took into their mouths all the banished and dirty words and tamed them and made them intimate. They overstepped, were son and daughter to each other, lovers, parents, all ways. They went back to all the places they'd met and had each other there, especially in the most terrible places, on the icy, bare ground, in the night. Grass began to grow. They went as far as they could go, to the very rim of the ravine, to a total possession that freed, and spoke of a child. In choppy sentences. So tiny, adorable, the bravest. Lively and smart. The most beloved. About a possible moment of redemption. They began resembling each other in the dark, traded eyes and mouths, mingled and fell asleep that way. She woke in the middle of the night. She went to the window and sat in the chair. In the glass she saw the reflection of her face, merging with the face of her father. Everything came back to her in a flash. How she'd given up on herself in order to be good, how she'd sobbed into her pillow, and how she filled in the hole. How, when she buried her father, she buried her mother, too, and how she had always been alone. Alone and good. And how badly she hated herself for wanting to live, and how she didn't have the knack. For living. And how never had she been able to budge the stone slab until this evening. It was heavy and cumbersome because the pit was omnipotent. It greedily guzzled love, promises, a young and lively boy, Marko's bottomless devotion. And nothing was enough for her; the pit was bottomless and more powerful than everything. He woke up not long after her. He rose quietly and hugged her from behind. Nora was across the river.

"Hey," he whispered and kissed her by her ear.

"You'll have to help me," she said to the window.

"I'll help you, whatever it takes; say the word."

"He can't—I want him gone; he doesn't deserve another day," she said coldly.

"Who are you talking about, Nora?"

"Please." She knocked him down on the spot.

"Nora, no. We're leaving here this moment. We'll leave all this behind. We'll be good." He kneeled before her. "My love . . ."

"I can't. My whole life, ours, all of it . . . you understand."

"I understand, but don't—you know I'd do anything . . ." His voice quavered. "I'd give you my heart."

"Just give me the number."

"Nora, don't do it, please; you'll destroy yourself. This is going nowhere."

"I cannot do it any other way."

He got up from the floor and began pacing back and forth

around the room, his hands over his temples. He looked over at Nora, naked, curled up by the window. Without her, in any case, nothing had meaning.

21.

Dum dum

I will hate icy cold
with a heart cased in seven skins
I will shoot straight in the back
I am born to rule

now (fall 2010)

The pressure nearly thrust his eyes from their sockets. His tongue went blue and sagged in the corner of his mouth; his spit swung from his chin to his neck when the metal bar with weights on the ends pressed him across the throat. It stopped the flow of oxygen, first to his lungs and then slowly to his brain, and the internal organs, all the way to the tips of his fingers. The last to go was his sense of hearing. He heard the thrum of the ventilation system, the radio jingles over the loud speakers, tambura players, festivities, shrieks, then silence, thrum, why, who, Kirin, Plavno, the bells, calls for help from the garage, Mariška's jeers, the crackling of the flames, wind in the high tops of poplars, the dark. He was as strong as a horse, and Schweppes strangled him on his weight-lifting machine for an eternity. The dirtiest job of these last years. Everything had been urging him to leave as soon as he took care of the mayor, but he'd stayed a day more, hoping to see her. Meanwhile, after almost twenty years, quite by chance, at the cash register of a gas station, he ran into the reservist who'd saved his life back then. They recognized each other the same millisecond, pretending they'd never seen each other before. The next night, before dawn, just as he was getting ready to leave on a long vacation, Marko summoned him over the Spanish network. He'd accessed it the evening before while making arrangements for his return to Madrid. He hadn't expected Marko would contact him, and even less that he'd ask for a *favor*. He owed it, and he couldn't refuse; that would be beneath him. They got together early in the morning at the Štrand, along the riverbank, where Marko had gone fishing as a boy. The boats rocked in the shallow waters, enveloped in mist and dark, half submerged, the paint peeling, rusty. Schweppes's car was parked on the access path, its lights off. Marko went down to him on foot, and when Schweppes saw him coming he got out of the car and lit a cigarette.

"Hello."

"Well, finally." Schweppes nodded.

"Yes, finally." Marko glanced at him out of the corner of his eye.

"You've been here the whole time?"

"Yup. And you? What brought you back to these parts?"

"A gig. I should have been long gone by now. Yes?"

"Ilinčić."

"Ilinčić?" Schweppes was quite surprised, and then, barely visibly, he smiled.

"I have ten thousand, no more."

"This is me paying back my debt. We're good."

"He's alone at the gym, six a.m., every morning." Marko glanced at his watch. It was exactly five. Schweppes nodded, bemused.

"Ilinčić . . ." While he said the name pictures came back to him of his mentor, the man who brought him into the profession, who was responsible for his initiation, for his first murder. The killing of Kirin, the Osijek policeman, which released the genie from the bottle. When the accusations began raining down about adhesive tape and garages, doubting his loyalty and knowing that only Schweppes knew everything, Ilinčić thought the time had come to get rid of him, but Schweppes was too adept and had an animal's nose for caution. By then he'd already matured and had spun his own network of people and spies and he learned, in time, of what lay in wait. He found a way to twist the man's arm and save himself. He didn't hold this against the man, not much; he might have done the same thing himself, but still this burned him. Ilinčić had been the father he never had—the father he'd killed for, but still, a father, better any father than none. The king was now old, and too many people nursed grudges against him, and now it was up to Schweppes to do him in. There was something poetic in this, almost archetypically just.

"Well, okay, old man . . . I have a flight at noon. That does it, I hope, and we never have to see each other again."

"As far as I'm concerned," said Marko. Everything in him wanted to run from that place. "So, take care . . ." he added.

"Oh, I'd like to ask"—Schweppes stopped him—"what were you thinking then?"

"Then?"

"Yes, when you saved the convoy." He'd never been able to understand.

Marko stood, half facing him, staring pensively at the water. "It was pointless for you to be killed . . . so much senseless death." He turned away, and Schweppes watched his back. Marko lifted an arm as if in greeting, or farewell, or absolution, but Schweppes still didn't understand.

An hour after he parted ways with Marko, when he walked by the front desk into Ilinčić's gym, when Ilinčić spotted him, the expression on his face was a mixture of fear, surprise, disbelief, and a confused smile. Already panting, he was sitting, legs sprawled, at the weight-lifting machine. Schweppes came over to him, arms flung wide, a smile on his face; it had been more than ten years since they'd laid eyes on each other. They'd killed so many people together, done so much evil that neither of them could remain indifferent. There was something warm in the encounter. But something told Ilinčić this was a little early in the day for a visit, that Schweppes was no longer a kid, that he hadn't found Ilinčić just to say hi. The only thing he couldn't detect by intuition was *why*, or rather, *why now?*

"Hey, old man." Schweppes was the first to speak. "How long has it been?" Ilinčić was still holding the weight. He didn't react fast enough.

"To what do I owe the . . . ?" he asked, genuinely surprised.

"Let me help you." Schweppes stood over him and, straddling him, took the weight from his hands and abruptly pressed him down. Ilinčić struggled fiercely, but Schweppes was younger, stronger, more motivated. He pinned him down quickly and gave him no more wiggle room. Except for one question between the two so distant breaths.

"Why? Who?" Ilinčić gasped several moments before he died.

"Nora Kirin," was the last thing Schweppes said. He didn't hear the gunshot, all he felt was warmth gushing from his neck and down his back, his knees buckling, and a sudden lightness in his head. The waiter-receptionist clutched the pistol and through his small, yellowed teeth, hissed:

"You filthy piece of shit! And you would like to rule!"

❧   ❧   ❧

Platforms
today is tuesday
nowhere left to go

She'd never crossed over to the other side of the cemetery. Killed a few months after the end of the fighting in a drunken brawl, her father was buried as a fighter along what was known as Šajkača Avenue, named for a style of Serbian military cap, in a cemetery laid out in 1994 where seventeen demolished houses had once stood. After peaceful reintegration, the local authorities kept doing what they could to move the cemetery, explaining that it had not been set up according to regulation and was an affront to the victims. The huge cap-shaped šajkača symbols that had ornamented the gravestones were taken down, the graves redone, and the cemetery was annexed to the older, adjacent Orthodox cemetery. The owners of the demolished houses were compensated. The accounts were settled, but the hatred a constant. Olivera placed a rose by her father's name, and then, for the first time, went through the dense darkness over to the other side. She walked by 938 white stone crosses and stepped into the memorial burial ground of the defenders. She circled around and lost almost an hour looking for him. There were fresh flowers, a message, a candle with the tricolor Croatian flag and the red-and-white checkerboard. On the monument there was a photograph of him, with young face and broad shoulders in his uniform. Her son's visage decked out in enemy regalia. Back in those days there was a lot of drinking and madness, euphoria and nausea were part of everyday life, but her nausea, that morning, was different. After that, the sickness was like clockwork: as soon as she opened her eyes her stomach would turn inside out, and only then could she continue with her day. She soon confessed this to her father, she had no choice; her nose bled from the slap he gave her, she was barely able to keep her balance, and the next day she left for Mladenovac. She spent the days there shut up in the house, in a city where there was not the slightest hint that only an hour and a half away by car there were thousands of fresh corpses and concentration camps. The reality normal for the people in the city seemed monstruous. This was the weirdest part of all. She gave birth a few days after her father was killed—stabbed in the back during a saints' day celebration. Her aunt grabbed the baby with her big hands, wrapped it firmly like a mummy in a diaper, tore it from Olivera's arms, and urged her to go back to the city alone, without the child. Dejo didn't cry at all; his big dark eyes peered everywhere, and he made sounds only when he was hungry. The two women clashed more and more often. His aunt was always claiming he was hungry, until once they both grabbed for the little bundle at the same time and it slipped softly off the ottoman. Olivera leaped up, appalled, and lifted him from the floor, pushing the huge woman away with superhuman strength while one bare breast full of milk shone white, flopping over her shirt. She boarded a bus that day and went home. With her baby. She quickly found her footing, started her work with the butcher shops and made her way as a single mother.

Life in the city in ruins limped along. Only the most essential things were repaired; all the poverty-stricken people from the regions devasted by war in central Bosnia, Republika Srpska, SAO Krajina, Knin poured in like rivers. All the people who couldn't make a go of it anywhere else ended up here, and with their joint efforts they changed the faces, spirit, and atmosphere of the city. And they quaked in fear of vengeance, deeply aware that someone else's house could never become their own this way. The turning point didn't come with guns and trumpets but with ordinary signatures on a piece of paper. Hence the bitterness and vengeance didn't run rampant; instead they were left buried deep beneath the layers of consciousness, foundations, earth in amounts large enough to smolder for decades to come. She came across him in a photograph in the local papers. He was standing with several defenders and members of the housing commission in front of the entrance to the building where she lived, holding keys to the apartment he'd been awarded. When they ran into each other one morning in the parking lot while she was taking Dejo to school, he didn't recognize her straight away. She walked by him, and when she turned, her back rigid, she saw that he, too, had turned. His gaze struck her like lightning. She spent that night smoking by the window, thinking to write to her brother in Stockholm. She didn't. He looked straight through her each time until they'd walled off the past. Tacitly and irretrievably. They never greeted each other, behaving like people who are capable of separating from themselves and their past. For that very reason it never occurred to Ante that the brown-eyed gentle boy was his son, the offspring of those long-ago sessions of interrogation and drunken brawls in Begejci. The boy who would fire two or three shots into him and was deeply in love with his wife. Olivera placed the second rose on the gravestone and turned to find her way out of the cemetery. Not far from the tall iron gate stood two figures in the dark. Uncle Stanko, her father's colleague and war buddy, was leaning in close to a lithe, petite woman. They were deep in heated debate, not expecting there'd be anybody at this time of day at the cemetery. Brigita and Velimirović were discussing the terms for a joint coalition or collaboration, the constituting of the new city council if Brigita's party, as was more than likely, won control. Now that the mayor had been eliminated, the money from the lease of the port could be doled out to help them secure the votes they needed for their own unprofitable ventures, for them to reap the most and the city to receive the least. This was a bigger handout than what had come before. Velimirović was prepared to agree to everything, as long as he was part of the ruling platform. The greatest challenge and the most difficult piece from his side was to weather the shitstorm over the Cyrillic signage. This had to be handled as prudently as possible. They'd divvy up the city: *we get the cemeteries and the halo, you get a few street names and the experience of being part of Europe.* Play dumb and leave the hogs to devour each other; toss in the occasional media spin and soothe the dogs that were straining at their leashes. To pick up where they'd left off and insure more decades of hatred. In the darkness of the cemetery by the gate they began looking more and more like each other, their talons and fangs mingled.

22.

Weary

inhale me, exhale me
relax me, release me
bring me, take me
place me, leave me
leave me

now (fall 2010)

When he shut the door behind him she knew where he was going. Without a goodbye. He'd been texting before he left, perched on the edge of the bed, while the whole time under the skin of his face his jaw was tensing and releasing. She saw herself go over to him, stroke his hair, tuck her knee between his legs and take away his cell phone. She saw herself do this from the chair where she was sitting. But she did nothing, she didn't move, though she knew that only one tender gesture would have been enough for the earth to spin off on an entirely different orbit. She didn't have the strength for it, even if in her deepest self she wished she did. She had to keep her grip and do nothing; this was the easy way out—let him go so far away that he'd never come back. Once she was alone, she made the bed, tidied the desk, washed the dishes. Dawn. She folded his clothes and buried her nose in his shirt sleeves. For a long time she inhaled his scent; it took her back to a street, years ago, where chestnut trees bloomed, to the smell of her gray terrier's wet fur and roasting corn, and it made her think of all the shades of green of the river in August. In a flash she could see herself lying on a sofa, wearing his shirt, while outside a soft gloom settled, and his hand was resting on her belly, which was starting to swell. Even thinking this, risking so much, was unbearable. They'd have to take on the entire world. Sooner or later something would happen to one of them, and the rest of her life would be reduced to remembering and waiting. Plan B was more bearable; she'd chosen Plan B in advance. Now all she'd have to do was to live out the rest in a blur, and an end would come, as it always did. The amount of torment in life was always proportionate to the amount of earlier happiness; for happiness one needed courage, a touch of madness, and at least a small reserve of faith. But she'd long since spent whatever reserve of faith she had. She took a shower and dressed, opened his laptop, and went online. On YouTube she typed in "Ekatarina Velika, 'Love,'" pressed pause, and watched the words scroll up on the screen:

> *I've always slept*
> *with your name on my lips*
> *you've always slept*
> *with my name on your lips*

and wherever I go
your hand is in mine
and when I wish to speak
I say we

She walked out of the apartment. Slowly, to the police station. The city was stirring; children were going in their separate groups to their separate Serbian and Croatian schools, nuns were gathering out in front of the hospital again, meanwhile up on the second floor the doctors were sterilizing their instruments, on the bench at the bus station a drunk was dozing. Everything was the same as it ever was. At the entrance to the police station Inspector Grgić bumped into her, nearly knocking her down. When he saw who it was, he seemed to wake up.

"You, again!" he snapped. "Not now, I'm in a rush; I've had a report of a murder! Come back this afternoon." She stepped in front of him, blocking his way.

"I know," she said, looking him straight in the eye.

"Look, I've no time for nonsense right now!" He was irritated.

"I did not come with nonsense," she said quietly.

"Ma'am, the laptop can wait. Meanwhile it seems like everybody in the city is getting killed!" he shouted.

"Ilinčić. I know."

"What? What do you know? How?" he asked.

"May we step inside for a moment so I can tell you?" she asked in a low voice.

"Ohhh . . . wait." He took his cell phone from his pocket and swiveled away from her. "Go to the hotel; I'll be there in ten." Then he swiveled back:

"Right this way, but please, quick and to the point. Please." He was at his wit's end. Nora nodded. While they passed through the station waiting area, Melania Gmaz shot up out of one of the plastic chairs as soon as she spotted them.

"Pardon me! Pardon me!" she called as the two of them strode hurriedy to his office. Grgić did not slow his pace; he rolled his eyes and snarled:

"That woman's going to be the death of me . . ."

Melania would not relent; she kept yelling after him. "I don't think I told you everything! I've more proof! I saw . . ." Her voice faded as Grgić banged the door shut behind them. He practically shoved Nora into the chair across from him. With his left hand he rubbed his eyes.

"Quick and to the point," he repeated. Nora nodded.

"I ordered Ilinčić's murder," she said, enunciating every word. Grgić froze. His eyebrows knit, his mouth sagged open.

"Come again?"

"I ordered Ilinčić's murder," she said with the same quiet.

For a time Grgić stared at the floor, then he sighed and looked up.

"Why?"

"Because he killed my father," she answered with complete self-control.

"Good god . . ."

Nora sank into the chair and let all the weariness of the world wash over her.

❀　　❀　　❀

Boy from the water

water falls
on your eyes the color of honey
I'm the boy from the water
with track marks under my arm

The building of the bridge, celebrated with pork cracklings, brandy, and a circle dance on the muddy ground, had begun six years before; the ground was broken by the communications minister at the time, who announced that this was a vital traffic artery and a crucial part of the government's plan for the accelerated construction of a network of ring roads and interchanges connecting the state roads, highways, cities, airports, and commercial zones throughout Croatia in an effort to give the country a competitive edge. Three years later, the work on the one-thousand-foot-long four-lane colossus was completed. The builders could only access it on ladders, right up to their last day on the job. The bridge had not yet been opened to traffic because there were no roads leading to it in either direction, as if somebody from outer space had plunked it down over the river, hedged in by meadows and brambles on either side, as precise as a blunder. Fifty million kunas had been poured into the concrete structure. And to make any sense of it, with roads leading to it and from it, they'd now need five times that much. Nobody had a clue about any plans for the future. Meanwhile, instead of roads, mountains of construction waste piled up on either side of the bridge, dumped there, mainly asphalt but also other types of rubble. The high-priority project had turned into a scrap heap, and nobody except scavengers ever went there anymore: a few years back they'd harvested all the drainage grids and the copper grounding wire. The people living nearby complained that their houses had been flooded three times that year because of the bridge. The backstory to the bridge to nowhere included, among others things, the Golubica restaurant, owned by Ilinčić's sister, since the highway exit ramp was supposed to run right by it. There was also a vacation community where Ilinčić had arranged a weekend cottage for himself—all part of the plan for a modern artery that would link the city to the highway for Zagreb. The work was halted because a new minister took office. The investor ran short of funds, and the bridge was abandoned, suspended there magically between heaven and earth.

He left the car, with the key in the ignition, on the path by the meadow. Night was falling as Marko made his way through the brambles. His feet were soaked, and he tripped over holes in the soggy soil, while the bridge kept seeming farther away. After a half hour's trudge he finally reached gravel, stepping around large chunks of rubble. He climbed up onto the bridge over which no car had ever driven, onto the asphalt that shone in the moonlight, mirroring the dark, star-studded sky. Partway across the span he sat and lit a cigarette, stared into the black water beneath him, and remembered a summer's day at the pool many years before. He recalled his friend and his friend's younger brother, Dražen, who went missing that day. The first day of the end of the world as he knew it. He suddenly saw the figure of the scrawny little boy that muggy afternoon; all that was left behind were his wristwatch on the towel and his gnawed peach pits. They searched for him till morning, draining the pool dry, they split into groups and for days scoured all possible places around the city, suburbs, woods. He was also at his friend's house when the police came to the door a few days later and their mother's wails rang out from the living room. Something was crushed in them then. Individually, as a generation, universally. They gawked at each other, baffled by life and the forces arrayed against it. Every warm and carefree image of their shared childhood, from the community around them, the innocence they shared was seared on that day, never to return. Not long afterward, the war began. Then an endless nothing. And then Nora, and a past that never ends, then Ekatarina Velika, the music he always returned to, then the song "Love," one more magnificent ruse of life after his existence in the safe haven he'd built for himself by giving up. And in the end, the black, black water, like the beginning and end of all things. A circle. He stubbed out the ember of his cigarette onto the thousands of grains of sand encased in the concrete of the bridge to nowhere, breathed deeply once more, thought about the boy, then about himself, then her, and dropped into the water.

23.

This is the country for us

this is the country for us
this is the country for all our people
this is home for us
this is home for all our children

now (fall 2010)

"Darling . . . my little darling . . ." she whispered, squeezing her fingers in her own, "my little girl . . ." Nora pulled her hands away, and her mother snatched them back and pulled them to her, wanting to hold on as long as possible, forever, bringing her face to the wet knot of their fingers.

"Don't, Mama," said Nora flatly.

"What have they done to you?" she asked, expecting no answer. After turning herself in to the police, Nora was remanded to detention, where she was held for a month on the suspicion that she'd organized and ordered the murder of Josip Ilinčić, city councillor and respected local politician. Since she'd confessed to her guilt, the investigation wrapped up quickly, and Nora was sentenced to live out her life at the women's prison in Požega. She reached her mother after she'd admitted everything. She hadn't wanted to see her until then. She didn't want to see her now. There was no longer a heart there to be broken, but she knew her mother's desire. In those last few months, Nora's mother had lost twenty pounds and aged twenty years. They knew everything yet didn't know what to say to each other. Time was passing too slowly for Nora, too quickly for her mother. The prison policewoman retreated to the farthest corner of the room, immersed in her cell phone.

"I am sorry I wasn't strong enough," said her mother, staring at the floor.

"Mama, this is not your fault; you did the very best you could." A note of tenderness in Nora's voice now.

"If only I could shut my eyes, Nora," she said as she crossed her hands and looked upward towards the ceiling.

"It will pass, Mama, everything will pass . . ." Nora stood up and signaled to the policewoman. She nodded and started over towards them. Her mother leaped up and threw herself on Nora, and they stood there like that for a few seconds. And then Nora scraped her mother off of her in pieces that scattered all over the gray linoleum, and nobody would ever be able to collect them again. She went out into the corridor that led to the cells. She no longer felt anything; she was completely free. On her way down the corridor she suddenly spotted familiar light eyes. Kristina was walking toward her and, when she saw Nora, an expression of surprise flashed across her impassive face.

"What are you doing here?" she asked, astonished.

"What does it look like?" said Nora. They stopped, and the policewoman let them.

"Huh," smirked Kristina, not expecting any further explanation. "Well, well." She nodded, almost with sympathy. "It's not much worse than outside, once you get the hang of it. The same maniacs, the same rules . . . just less space . . . And your right buttock gets stronger than your left when you go out for your walk, because they always have you walk the circle in the same direction . . . And you use a lot of water when you're on the toilet, too much. There's no privacy, so everyone runs the tap so others can't hear it when you're taking a shit. But . . . people do that outside, too, don't they?" Kristina patted Nora on the shoulder. Nora just nodded. There was something perfectly precise in Kristina's universal truths about the outside and inside worlds. There were many more years for her to ponder these things, to fashion her stoicism, learn not to wish for more than what was given. The policewoman hurried her along to her cell, and Nora obeyed her without a word. She stepped in and the door closed behind her. She'd be able to manage. After all, there was nothing more for her to do, nor did she need anything. She was prepared to make her peace with everything. Nothing was so terrible anymore, except maybe for one thing: realizing you can't open the door from the inside.

TRANSLATOR'S NOTE

Images of "holes" and "pits" pervade this political thriller. Indeed the title of the novel in its Croatian edition, *Rupa*, means "Hole." The city of Vukovar, referred to only as "the city" throughout, is one such hole; the pits into which the victims of the massacres were thrown during the eighty-seven-day siege are another, as are the wounds of the people of Vukovar.

Vukovar is situated at Croatia's easternmost periphery, across the Danube River from Serbia. During the 1990s, ex-Yugoslavia was rocked by a series of savage wars. Early on, in the fall of 1991, Vukovar was besieged by the joint forces of the Yugoslav People's Army and Serbian paramilitaries; the siege reduced the Baroque city to rubble, and when the paramilitaries and army forces broke the siege and swarmed the city, they massacred hundreds of people, most of them Croats. These massacres served as the basis for three of the trials held at the International Criminal Tribunal for the former Yugoslavia, two of which never reached completion due to the deaths of the defendants.

After they broke the siege, a Serbian territorial authority asserted control and occupied the city; only after lengthy negotiations in 1998 was the city reincorporated into Croatia during the period known as the "peaceful reintegration." At that time, many local Croats moved back to their Vukovar homes and were reinstated as the majority community, while the community of Serbs who stayed on to share Vukovar with the returning Croats were accorded minority status. To this day, the elementary and secondary schools are segregated: the Serbian schoolchildren are taught according to the curriculum used in Serbia, while Croatian schoolchildren follow the curriculum used throughout the schools of Croatia.

In Croatia, Vukovar and the siege have become a tragic, almost sacred, symbol of the war, but because the city is far from Zagreb, Croatia's capital city, the country's focus is elsewhere most of the time. *We Trade Our Night for Someone Else's Day* provoked a raging controversy after it came out in 2016 because it exposes the venality, the cynicism, and the tragedy of Vukovar—and, by extension, of the people of the former Yugoslavia generally, a tragedy that can no longer be ascribed to an external enemy.

All the titles and epigraphs at the beginning of chapters and sections within chapters are from songs by the Yugoslav band Ekatarina Velika, also known as EKV. The band's sound, themes, and feel are reminiscent of the Velvet Underground and Nirvana. They are one of the last Yugoslav bands before what had been Yugoslavia until 1990 broke up into eight successor states, so these songs represent a precious poetic document for Nora's and Marko's generation that was lost in the vortex of the war, displacement, emigration. Here are the songs, with their original titles, so interested readers can find them online:

"Hands"	"Ruke"
"Forget This City"	"Zaboravi ovaj grad"
"Someone's Watching Us"	"Neko nas posmatra"
"The Real World around Me"	"Stvaran svet oko mene"
"Moving Toward"	"Kad krenem ka"
"Years of Lead"	"Olovne godine"
"We're Sinking"	"Tonemo"
"Be Alone on the Street"	"Budi sam na ulici"
"Like It Used to Be"	"Kao da je bilo nekad"
"She and He and He and I"	"Ona i on i on i ja"
"Money in Hands"	"Novac u rukama"
"Into Darkness We Run"	"Bežimo u mrak"
"Blue and Green"	"Modro i zeleno"
"A Few Years"	"Par godina za nas"
"Circle"	"Krug"
"Time to Cleanse"	"Treba da se čisti"
"Eyes the Color of Honey"	"Oči boje meda"
"Cold"	"Hladan"
"The First and the Last Day"	"Prvi i poslednji dan"
"Garden"	"Vrt"
"Hunger"	"Glad"
"People from the Cities"	"Ljudi iz gradova"
"The Ghetto"	"Geto"
"Hey, Mama"	"Hej, Mama"
"Synchro"	"Sinhro"
"Just a Couple of Years for Us"	"Par godina za nas"
"You Are All My Pain"	"Ti si sav moj bol"
"Dum dum"	"Dum dum"
"Platforms"	"Platforme"
"Weary"	"Umorna"
"Love"	"Ljubav"
"Boy from the Water"	"Dečak iz vode"
"This is the Country for Us"	"Ovo je zemlja za nas"

ELLEN ELIAS-BURSAĆ
Cambridge, MA

We Trade Our Night for Someone Else's Day **223**